Golden Handcuffs Review

Golden Handcuffs Review Publications

Seattle, Washington

Golden Handcuffs Review
Publications

Editor

Lou Rowan

Contributing Editors

Andrea Augé
Nancy Gaffield
Stacey Levine
Rick Moody
Toby Olson
Jerome Rothenberg
Scott Thurston
Carol Watts

LAYOUT MANAGEMENT BY PURE ENERGY PUBLISHING, SEATTLE

PUREENERGYPUB.WORDPRESS.COM

Libraries: *this is Volume II, #27.*

Information about subscriptions, donations, advertising at:
www.goldenhandcuffsreview.com

Or write to: Editor, Golden Handcuffs Review Publications
1825 NE 58th Street, Seattle, WA 98105-2440

In Memory
Robert C. Jones

Society pressures artists to camouflage the good time they are having. I come to my studio to paint for the sheer fun of it, for the sheer pleasure of trying to come up with something I've never seen before. And if I screw up, I don't screw up the universe or anyone else's life. There's a possibility for freedom in art that doesn't exist anywhere else in the world, and I love it.

Contents

THE WORK

Art

Robert C. Jones
Untitled, 1972, 26 x 30 inches, oil on canvas.
Courtesy of G. Gibson Gallery, Seattle WA . . . . cover

Fiction

Toby Olson
The Sister and the Cistern 17
Sex 21

Mark Axelrod-Sokolov
from The Mad Diary of Malcolm Malarkey, Phd. 31

Alan Singer
Audience 44

Poetry

Fanny Howe
4 Poems 53

Peter Hughes
Cant 57

Meredith Quartermain
8 Poems 61

Jake Marmer
5 Poems 71

Aidan Semmens
    5 Poems 80

Philip Terry
    from Dante's Purgatorio Canto XX 91

Kat Peddie
    13 Ways of Looking at the Lives of the Artists 97

Toby Olson
    Disturbed 101

Lissa Wolsak
    from Lightsail 109

Sarah Hayden
    S1: Holt 117

Daphne Marlatt
    3 Poems 125

Tania Hershman
    3 Poems 131

Marilyn Stablein
    Toasters 134

Essays

Ian Brinton
    Breaking Out (on Michael Rumaker, Black Mountain) 7
    Outside/Inside (on Martha King) 138

Sara Wilson
    "through my hand to you": Hank Lazer's Brush Mind: At Hand . . 143
    Interview with Hank Lazer 150

Augustus Young
    'In His Rightful Garden': Anthony Rudolf, the Poet 157

NOTES ON CONTRIBUTORS 165

Breaking Out

Ian Brinton

When Michael Rumaker was kicked out of his home in Gloucester County, south of the Delaware River, in 1950 it was an expulsion directed by his father and with his mother's tacit assent. It was for not going to church and for being queer. A year later he heard Ben Shahn give a lecture at the Philadelphia Museum of Art extolling the virtues of the unconventional and innovative educational establishment in the western hills of North Carolina: Black Mountain College. Arriving on a work scholarship in 1952 he later recorded his initial reactions:

> The place was in many ways just as I had envisioned it:
> steep mountains with isolated buildings along the slopes, a
> sense of vast wilderness-like space and isolation.

Soon picking up on the unusual sense of educational space being provided he "also recognized, with a delicious excitement of my well-hidden but naturally rebellious heart, that there was something going on in this isolated backwoods called Black Mountain College that I had never conceived of in the world outside." Going on to describe how he learned his first lesson at Black Mountain he remembered "When confronted with objects of creation beyond my comprehension to keep my mouth firmly shut and my eyes and ears open." The latter part of that observation he kept firmly to throughout his writing career. Travelling into Ashville with Charles and Connie Olson on the first Friday night after starting he felt that "maybe here I could finally learn to write; equally as important, maybe here I could find a place to be."

The first real advice that Olson offered the young Rumaker was to saturate himself in Theodore Dreiser, "Saturate yourself in Sherwood Anderson for the limpidity of his style, and Stephen Crane", emphasizing Crane's short story 'The Blue Hotel', "the best thing he ever did." As a result of this directive Rumaker later recorded that much of his early time at Black Mountain was spent in this process of elimination:

> Through Charles's encouragement, of pushing me back
> to myself, to what was my experiential truth, I'd begun
> early that summer of 1953 to write from that experience,
> particularly about my family....Charles picked up on these
> first-hand experiences, and bid me to *mine* them.

And that was the direction, "direct, clean, and to the point, a precise, uncluttered image." It was only later, after his first public reading that he overheard the music teacher, Stefan Wolpe, say to Olson "The trouble with Rumaker is he doesn't know how to *lie* yet". The lie of the imagination creates the truth of reality. Or, as Charles Tomlinson, the first poet to really introduce the Black Mountain poets to an English audience, put it in 1956, "The artist lies / For the improvement of truth. Believe him."

The first serious story that Rumaker wrote was 'The Truck':

> It was in the autumn, in the midst of all the uncertainties
> about the future of the college, after two years of continued
> false starts and superficial scratchings, that I wrote my
> first real short story, although, in what was to become
> usual for me, I didn't know it till after the fact. Heeding
> Charles's advice, what I did to get it was reach back into my
> adolescence in the mid-1940s to a street gang I got to know
> through a childhood pal, a former next-door neighbor, who

had moved with his family from our sleepy little South Jersey town to the northern section of Camden, in a tough, working-class neighborhood…Looking back on it, writing 'The Truck' had been my first totally pleasurable writing experience, something Charles told us *writing should be*, a terrific sense of enjoyment in the first-time experience of words as *living* things, of letting go and letting form grow out of content, as Olson, via Creeley, suggested. With the response of Olson and the others to back me, I felt the possibilities of really becoming a writer at last. In their eyes, and starting in my own, I was beginning to smarten up, learning to *lie*.

Olson's description of Rumaker's new stories was overheard at the Thanksgiving dinner at Meadows Inn in 1954. Mike Rumaker had been a student there for two years:

> I was just talking about your new stories, Mike, and how each word is sharp, is like cutting words out of metal with shears.

'The Truck' was sent off to Robert Creeley in Mallorca where he was editing *The Black Mountain Review* and in October that year Creeley wrote back accepting it for issue 5 of the magazine where it appeared in the summer of 1955 alongside work by Joel Oppenheimer, Robert Duncan, Louis Zukofsky, Jonathan Williams, Charles Olson, William Bronk, Robert Creeley and Denise Levertov.
Whilst staying in New York in the winter of 1954 Rumaker hitched home to see his family:

> It took me most of the day, getting short hops from exit to exit, to finally arrive at Exit 3, where I got off to head for my hometown of National Park a few miles distant. As I was hurrying along in the now-darkness along the winding exit ramp of the Turnpike, I encountered a car full of drunken servicemen travelling up from their base in the South, on leave to spend the holidays home. One of them was a marine with a bandaged hand who was more drunk than the others and who lived, as it turned out, in my hometown, and who the driver of the car, a young soldier, sick of him, was

trying to dump on me. I took notes in my head of all the vivid details of that experience for future use.

The first draft of this story was written between Christmas and New Year in New York, 1954 although it didn't appear in *Evergreen Review* until the summer of 1958 where it sat alongside Beckett's 'Krapp's Last Tape' and Olson's 'Human Universe'. Introducing the first Grove Press collection of Rumaker's stories collected under the title *Gringos*, 1966, Gilbert Sorrentino wrote that unlike many of the characters in the world of American 'dirty realism' Rumaker's people are *irretrievably* lost, lost in a sense that recalls the world of Dante's *Inferno*:

> His characters are located in a relentless present, spatially undifferentiated, except insofar as their places are either starkly public or wholly empty. The one constant in these narratives is that everyone is defined by despair. The condition of despair cannot be ameliorated, and the America so defined by these lost souls is a cruel and empty one.

Rumaker's story opens with a placing within landscape that draws the reader in:

> The tractor-and-trailer rolled slowly off the shoulder and onto the turnpike, its red and yellow lights blinking. Jim stood a minute watching it go, then leaned down and picked up his suitcase and started walking briskly along the exit road, past the brightly lighted toll booths. He walked faster, tucking his scarf tightly about his throat as a cold wind sprang up. The exit road made a sweeping curve downward, joining the main highway a hundred yards on. He shifted his suitcase to the other hand and headed toward the highway. As he walked along a Chevrolet convertible pulled up beside him, the motor idling. The horn blew. Jim turned, staring blindly into the headlights, and kept on going. The horn blew again, the car inching alongside him. The window of the driver's side rolled down and a head poked out.
> "Hey, buddy. C'mere.

The desolate atmosphere of the uninhabited wasteland associated with a motorway exit route is created immediately with the opening image of desertion. The heavy vehicle has left the hitch-hiker at exit three and we can feel the isolation as it "rolled slowly off" the stopping point and "onto the turnpike". The blinking of the lights seems like the last communication from a civilization in movement which has left a refugee stranded. The blinding headlights of the car which pulls up beside Jim usher in an inescapable world of personal involvement which will soon become nightmarish in its confusion of violence and homo-erotic responsibilities. The car unloads a drunken marine and Jim is trapped into being responsible for him "as the tail lights of the convertible disappeared in the traffic." The marine's hand is "crudely wrapped in a dirty handkerchief damp with blood" and his explanation is

> "Window!" laughed the marine, his head flopping on his chest. "Doggie. Only he was on'a other side'a window... smashed...". His head flew back and he shouted, "Smashed the fucking doggie!"

This violent sense of achievement at having attacked the US soldier (the term "doggie" pre-dates Hubert Selby's use of it in the opening section of *Last Exit to Brooklyn*) is linked with breaking a window and it is in this image, associated with the military 'glass house', that we see the helpless terror of the man who is trying to escape from his own world of self-doubt. The self-doubt is reflective of unresolved feelings concerning male homosexuality as the marine cannot move away from the image of his own actions:

> "I smashed his face," he moaned. "Cut it all up. I showed him. Cut his face to ribbons. Ground his face in the broken glass. He won't make faces any more. I ground his pretty face to bits."

The word "pretty" and the flirtatious associations of making faces sit uneasily with the brutality of the memory and the lonely caged figure of the marine who cannot break out of the constricted world of American homophobia. He veers between calling Jim "babydoll" and "a real buddy" before confronting three soldiers who are out for the night, provoking a fight that leaves him "the prostrate figure" at the end, presumably dead. The isolation of the marine, named Stark, the man who feels that he is in a glass house, is moved into the foreground of the story as Jim supports him off the road in search of a telephone booth so that Stark's father can be contacted to pick him up at exit three. The confused telephone conversation with Jim attempting to locate the father emphasises even more the complete loneliness of these figures; it is clear that no one is coming to pick up, rescue or heal the damaged marine. As Jim helps him across a road they glimpse what it might be like to be on the other side of the glass:

> They crossed tree-lined streets, the trees slender and bare in winter, and on either side, stretching down the blocks, low bungalows with warm yellow lights glowing in the windows. "Pretty. Awful pretty," croaked the marine, swinging his head from left to right. "Ain't it pretty, buddy?"

Left propped up against a sheer wall of plate-glass belonging to a drugstore while Jim goes to search for a taxi the marine can only say "I'll bust it. Bust any window I see…Bust the doggie." As Jim finally gets through to a taxi firm the marine makes a desperate attempt to smash the plate-glass of the store with his "bloody hand lifted high over his head, clenched as a fist":

> The glass shuddered under the impact. He threw back his arm and pounded the window a second time, leaving a smear of blood where his fist struck.

The world of the 'glass-house', resembling in its sense of a penitentiary the power games exploited in the creation of Panopticon-style prisons, is central to Ken Kesey's 1962 novel *One Flew Over the Cuckoo's Nest*. There the Big Burse's central observation tower protects her sanity, the correct way of perceiving reality according to the Combine of Political Power, differentiated from the madness of the inmates, by means of a highly polished sheet of glass. The narrator, Chief Bromden, acts as our guide to this Hell where Big Nurse spends the day sitting at her desk and looking out of her window and making notes on what goes on out in front of her. The anarchic inmate Randall P. McMurphy confronts her power by running his hand through the glass barrier:

> The glass came apart like water splashing, and the nurse threw her hands to her ears. He got one of the cartons of cigarettes with his name on it and took out a pack, then put it back and turned to where the Big Nurse was sitting like a chalk statue and very tenderly went to bushing the slivers of glass off her hat and shoulders.
> "I'm sure *sorry,* ma'am," he said. "Gawd but I am. That window glass was so spick and span I com-*pletely* forgot it was there."

Unlike the heroic MacMurphy whose style is modelled on the Wild West Cowboy, Rumaker's isolated marine can never break through or out: as he lies "stretched out a little distance from the drugstore" the owner comes out with a sponge and a tin of water. For a brief moment the reader might wonder if there could be an act of compassion from a Samaritan before realising that she is there to just clean up that window again:

> She rubbed briskly, pausing once to dip the sponge again in the water and wring it out, then polished the glass clean with a corner of her apron.

In the 1966 Penguin selection of Rumaker's work the editor, Tony Goodwin, chose a cover which depicted a manic figure whose fist is punching glass only to crack it not break it. It was the first photograph cover that Penguin used and it cost Goodwin his job!

When Rumaker finished his three years at Black Mountain College he went to live for a time in San Francisco and the world of tacit segregation haunting the place in the late 50s was presented in terrifying detail in his memoir of Robert Duncan. After describing a scene in the cellar of a downtown bar that could have illustrated a landscape from Dante Rumaker found himself passing by the alley between City Lights Bookshop and the Vesuvio Bar on Columbus Avenue:

> I saw half a dozen young men standing up on the front and

back seats of an open convertible jammed in that narrow place, their bodies swaying silently back and forth, going at each other with broken beer bottles.

George Butterick, had referred to 'Exit 3' as "being *on the road* in a desolate landscape charted only by impersonal traffic signs". It was Charles Olson who had played the role of teacher, traffic officer, to the young Rumaker and in *Black Mountain Days* the student recorded the importance of what had taken place:

> What Olson had been trying to pound into my head – into all our heads – was, for starters, to write, simply, what we knew from our own experience, what we had seen with our own eyes, what we had heard with our own ears, to write it in our own tongue, "like Pausanias", the ancient Greek traveller and geographer, he'd instruct us, "go out and see for yourself and come back and tell what you saw and heard, first-hand." And this I found was the hardest thing to do for a variety of reasons: fear of exposure, of plunging into the imagination, the main ones; fear of facing not only the world but myself, another. The gist of it was to get the cataracts out of my eyes, unplug my ears, and speak direct with a singular voice – "the many in one" – rather than mouthing the stolen, second and third-hand banalities of others, including my mother's.

It was Olson who some months after Rumaker graduated from Black Mountain wrote 'As the Dead Prey Upon Us' with its urgent cry to "disentangle the nets of being" in order to take responsibility for living a life that reaches beyond our inheritances. The poem recognises that "Purity / is only an instant of being" and that "the trammels / recur". Rumaker's early prose inhabits this world of purity and it threads its way through the eight dream pieces he gave to John Wieners for the second issue of the magazine *Measure* which appeared from Boston in 1958. Olson was struck by Rumaker's interest in the clarity of dream sequences and sent him a copy of his own poem, 'The Librarian' in late January 1957, the day it had been written, outlining his own position in the accompanying letter:

It raises the whole problem of how one gets dream material to avoid its own obviousness. And I take it the rule is the turning of it – drying of it out, shifting it into the real – has to be done by a means of the poem itself, not by exterior devices.

Rumaker wrote a short piece on 'The use of the unconscious' for that issue of *Measure* looking at a vivid approach to the interleaving of landscape and imagination:

Story can be, obliquely, a map of the unconscious, its terrain and peopling.
The physical can be made to yield psychic responses.
The unconscious nests the actual.

In the fall of 1958 Rumaker entered the Rockland Psychiatric Center, whose name in Ginsberg's *Howl* represented one of the ways a repressive society had attempted to destroy the best minds of a generation and he wrote to Duncan in September the following year "I want to smash everything. I want to smash these gray clerks of the soul. I want the day back. I am not a psychopath. I am not nuts." Some of his experiences in Rockland found their way into his first novel, *The Butterfly*, which centred on the affair he had with Yoko Ono before she became associated with John Lennon. In the isolated Hell of the Center which has become Home, the main character, another Jim, "kept his eyes averted as they walked past the buildings on either side of the street. He stared at the ground, not liking to see the other patients locked in on the porches. That always made his heart sink, made him get depressed. Some of the patients were pacing rapidly back and forth, while others stood mute and alone, lost in some profound and unknowable silence. They each seemed alone, each cut off from the other and from the life about them." One of his friends in the Home which he is about to leave clenches his teeth "and swung to the window and smashed the screen with his fist. The impact made a blunt dead sound. The screen was unyielding, as though it had not been touched."

In *Robert Duncan in San Francisco*, republished five years ago by City Lights Press and edited by Ammiel Alcalay and Megan Paslawski the closing pages of the narrative visit the time of

Rumaker's discharge from Rockland. Trying to remember how to live an un-institutionalized life he wrote to Duncan on January 4th 1961:

> Dear Robert
> I have re-read your letters, letters I scarcely remember.
> I have been so withdrawn at Rockland and buried under
> the river of my life. Now I find them filled with kindnesses
> I cherish. They are dear to me…Your dark and splendid
> sensuality has always been foreign to me. I'm a seed
> feather. Which also has its splendours and toughness. It
> endures as well. It's only that we each, in our own way, work
> the making of a world.

Ken Kesey's version of smashing that plate glass window reflects an uplifting and sentimental denouement to the world of Big Nurse. Chief Bromden picks up an enormous control panel from the patients' tub room and hurls it through the screen:

> The glass splashed out in the moon, like a bright cold water
> baptizing the sleeping earth.

Bromden runs for it and escapes hitching a lift going north in a truck full of sheep and the novel concludes "I been away a long time."

For Michael Rumaker bringing it all clear to mind was the result of his experience at Black Mountain College. As he wrote to Duncan on April 4th 1956:

> I went there wanting something. And found it.

The Sister
and the Cistern

Toby Olson

Devout Princes of the May, you might say, but there were a few problems. She was flirty. And she had a way with pleats and draping. She even washed her starched white wimple, that stiff half-moon wafer covering most of her chest, in some substance that gave it a third dimension. Sill white, but if you lowered your gaze from her beautiful face, her crisp white bandeau dressing her forehead like a bandana worn by a sorcerer, you would find you were seeing deep into some unearthly presence of dark clouds and rain. And at night you might even see stars.

Sister Mary Grace, just two years out of the convent in Guadalajara Mexico, now teaching mathematics to high school seniors at Saint Lois catholic school. Saint Lois was not really a saint, but the grandmother of one, Timothy, whom she had instructed. Grandmothers are always sainted. This sister was only a few years older than her students.

And she was excited by them, the energy of the young, and yes, their sexuality. She was feeling it, this late adolescent randyness, and she recognized she'd never had an adolescence of her own. When she came to America, she noticed that many nuns were out of habit and were like ordinary women, and this frightened her, so she quickly decided that she would always wear her habit, slightly refined of course, and she did.

In the convent dormitory, the nuns were goofing around, playing grabass, farting to excessive laughter, generally on the loose. It had been May Day at the school, little teaching, but a good deal of policing, keeping the kids corralled and out of trouble. An exhausting eight hours, and now habits had been shed, and the six sisters were romping around in their underwear. The seventh sister, Mary Grace, was not among them, but was ensconced in her small room, a cell really, preparing for her appointment. The first and the last time, she thought. Just this once. I've never....

First her cotton underwear and black stockings, then her long black dress, which she had hemmed so that her shoes, a little higher of heel than the usual, would show. Her woven belt, the rosary, then a good deal of time spent with her coif, her bandeau, and the black veil flowing down her back. Then her wimple of course, freshly washed and treated, so that this time ghostly figures, very much like tortured saints, danced in a gloom. What foolishness, she thought. Just this once. Just this once. She wasn't looking for love.

Mary Grace grew up on a farm far from the city of Merida, on the Yucatan peninsula, and so she was comfortable in the town where she taught, since it was surrounded by farmland, woods and low hills. On her father's farm she'd worked the crops and was home-schooled. The work was hard, but her father was a kind man, and she had plenty of time for her carving, those small sainted figures she had fashioned even as a small child, learning technique from a Mayan worker her father employed to help with the harvesting.

And she was very good at it, producing a series of saints that dressed the shelves and mantle in their farm house. These would be given as gifts to those her father did business with. They were always delighted with the craftsmanship. And she had continued with this endeavor when older, carving the figures of people she knew, nuns at the convent where she had taken her vows, prizes given to those American students who excelled on various tests and oral presentations, here, in her new life.

Now she slipped the small carved figure into the pocket of her dress. She was ready. It was seven o'clock, and not quite dark, and she left the convent dorm to the frolicking nuns, and set out for her rendezvous.

Father John the Baptist Esposito, known throughout the parish as Johnny E, had become a raconteur, though he had started out as a saintly presence, taking on the task of teaching disabled children when all others shunned them. He'd been sweet and dignified, and everyone, including the young parish mothers, loved him.

He was forty-two years old now. He told entertaining stories and jokes, drank a good deal, gambled at the Seminole casino a few towns away, and had an eye for the ladies, at times, it was rumored, taking their love for him quite literally and acting upon it. Somewhere, deep in his head or his loins or his conscience, he may have regretted what he had become, shameful, hardly a real priest at all, but he was unaware of this and felt it was right to enjoy the life he had chosen for himself. He seldom prayed anymore, and when he said Mass the words came only from memory, not devotion. He had no place in his heart for Jesus.

And so it was that he found pleasure in the face and figure of Sister Mary Grace, the nun he saw often in his perambulations at the high school. He taught Bible studies there, a required course that the students had little taste for and neither did he. He knew his Bible, but he was no longer interested in it, and his teaching was little more than rote.

They spoke a few times, the good sister querying him about Biblical matters and he taking in her beauty. And after a while their talk moved on to secular subjects, movies she had never seen, the pleasure of alcoholic beverages, current fashions in women's clothing. There was a beautiful place in the hills outside of town, he told her, smiling a little lasciviously. She might enjoy it. They could meet there. He would bring something to eat and some wine.

And so it was that Sister Mary Grace headed into the hills on a well worn path as daylight faded and the stars came out. There was no breeze, and a bright sliver of moon hung in the clear sky.

And Johnny E was waiting there, sitting on the smooth concrete edge of the large cistern that provided rainwater for irrigation of the fields below. The cistern was full, the deep dark water rising almost to the lip of the low rectangular wall that contained it.

She sat down beside him, her black dress rising a little to reveal her slim, perfectly formed calves. He touched her fingers as he handed her a glass of wine, which she sipped with little pleasure, though she enjoyed the few cold shrimp he presented on a glass plate over a thin bed of Boston lettuce. There were nuts too, just a few, and pita bread. They ate and talked, and he looked into her dark, inviting eyes, and just as he was preparing to move closer, to possibly kiss her to get things started, she reached into her dress pocket and presented him with the small carved figure she had fashioned.

It was him, the man he once was, as seen through her innocent eyes, this beautiful nun. And it accused him. The figure's head was lowered in profound prayer, and a rosary fell from its delicately carved fingers. My fingers, he thought, my losses.

He knew he couldn't go back, couldn't be the real priest he had once been. Though he still wore the clothing of his order, it was only a disguise. He was a charlatan.

But what to do? She was here now, smiling at him. Beckoning him? No, he thought, for in her eyes he saw her purity of spirit, her saintliness. She had been tempted, perhaps by the devil, but she had found energy and peace in her virginity. Now it was locked up tight, beyond any soiling or violation. Yet he knew he wanted her, and this want was yet another reminded of what he had become. She was the object of his evil desires, and he knew he must rid himself of her.

He pulled her toward him, kissed her stony lips, then pushed her back over and into the cistern.

There had been no lakes or ponds or other watering holes on the Yucatan farm where she had been raised, and she had never learned to swim, but for awhile she managed to stay afloat, to look up at him in this baptism, her eyes aglow in her faith and the saintly figures on her wimple accusing him. Then she slipped below the surface, followed by her veil, that floated on the water for a long moment and then was gone under with her.

He sat there for awhile, considering what he'd done. Then he stood up, danced in place for a moment, settling his genitals, and headed down the path with the remaining foodstuffs. The miniature rendering floated on the surface above the dear sister.

She had been his nemesis, his shocking reminder of what had been and was now gone. She had been no saint. He was sure of that. But she had been a very good girl.

Sex

Toby Olson

I've always had trouble with my name. It's not that I don't like it, nor do I spend much time considering it, but when I find occasion to speak it, in introduction, announcement, or even simple identification, the letters forming the two words feel foreign in my mouth and are not familiarly articulated, so that those who might write it down often misspell it, placing an e where an o belongs, an s instead of a z.

The reason for this awkward glossolalia, though unclear, has led me to other considerations, such as those dealing with aliases and pen-names, and most recently gender reassignments. What happens, for example when Karl Hulse becomes Carla Hulse or, more extremely, when Caroline become Gunther?

If the identification is made early in life, then it might be that the male appellation that hides the true female one, Freddy and Barbra, becomes foreign in the mouth, but if Barbra is only hinted at vaguely as a future possibility, then it too might be spoken, privately I assume, in a language awkwardly foreign. But names are only the tip of the iceberg, so to speak.

In a recent discussion with a friend who insisted that sexual reassignment surgery should not be covered by either the government, through Medicare and Medicaid, or by insurance companies, I pointed out that plastic surgery, when elective, was at this point not covered, and that it might be usefull to compare the two.

With few exceptions, such as breast augmentation, elective plastic surgery is for the most part diminishment. Face, neck, and other body parts are carved away. Care, brought about by years of living, is carved away, and wrinkles, sagging cheeks and eye bags are made to disappear, so that the figure is returned to an earlier time in a kind of cleansing by retrogression, a time in which internal sexuality is seen once again on the surface, or if sexual vibrancy had been lost, it was now back again, and one could enter the world as the one who once had it or had at least wished for it. This returning, which is a choice, does not come cheaply, neither psychologically nor financially, and choice, when it comes to the latter, is not covered by insurance.

Is gender reassignment surgery a choice? My interlocutor must be proposing that it is, and thus should not be covered. And yet, for the subject of such surgery -Karl to Carla, Caroline to Gunther-, such reassignment is a necessity, a movement from the inauthentic to the appropriate. The subject of plastic surgery returns to an earlier self, the reassigned to the authentic one, so that Carla and Gunther can participate in the world as who they are and not flounder there as fakes of real persons, and so for the good of society gender reassignment surgery should be covered by insurance and elective plastic surgery, an ego driven choice presenting to the world a fake youthfulness, should not.

My argument is for the most part of course a shaky political one that has to do with liberation, and sexual liberation has been a concern of mine for many years, ever since I discovered I was Consuela in the body of Javier and accomplished, at no small expense, the change. I was only nineteen at the time, and while in recovery, I began a study of various sexual anomalies. I read Krafft-Ebing, Lenz and Kinsey, looked into Magnus Kirschfeld, and even examined various forms of pornography and molestation. Then I entered college, receiving a degree in experimental psychology and one in social work. I'm thirty-six at the present writing and have for five years now been a board certified sexual therapist practicing under the name of Doctor Consuela Lopez. My doctorate was acquired through the mail, and though I am a woman of Latin origin, most of my patients are gringos.

Here, then, I present three of my case histories. I've selected these because thinking of them still gives me professional pleasure. I have of course changed the patients' names and have included my own comments, to give flavor to the narratives, in brackets.

Edward Colcheck was a thirty-five year old accountant, a large man who obviously spent a good deal of time behind his desk. He was soft in body and sported a significant paunch, and he seemed to be somewhat out of breath when he arrived. I ushered him into the easy chair across from my desk, where he sunk into the leather cushions, and studied his face in order to ascertain a hint of his character. He seemed at ease, though I suspected that, at any moment, he might turn belligerent.

"So why have you come here?"

"Well, there's really nothing wrong. It's just that my wife thought it might be a good idea."

"And?" [I was drawing him out]

"It's the sex, I guess. I like to do it under the bed."

"Doesn't it get crowded down there?" [*Ay, Caramba!* I thought]

"It's only me and my wife!" [Here was that belligerence]

"No, no! I meant the space. Isn't it a little tight?"

"I would call it cozy."

"I can see that, cozy. But what about your wife? She sent you here after all." [I was prodding him.]

"I came of my own free will." [His tone was cold, almost accusatory.]

"I'm asking about your wife."

"Well she does it, you know. But she really doesn't like it. She's bigger than me, and she hits her head on occasion."

"On the floor?"

"No. On the slats. It's a platform bed."

"So, she is on top?" [I could see a hint of embarrassment in his eyes. He feared the coming sex talk.]

"Yes, that's true. I feel protected that way, covered."

"Do you undress under there?"

"No, no! We put our clothes on top of the bed. The lights are off."

"So you really don't see each other."

"No, but we feel each other."

"Are you sure? Given the tightness, maybe you're feeling yourself."

[He hesitated, having no answer for that.]

"I want you to try something," I said. "I want you to plug in a night-light. Then only get under the bed up to your necks, both of you. Make sure she can see your face and you can see hers."

"I don't have such a light."

"Buy one."

He returned a week later.

"Well?"

"It was okay, her face and all. But she caught her nightgown on one of the slats and ripped it. It was her favorite."

"But you said you put your clothing on top of the bed!" [I spoke in a surprised way.]

"Nightgowns! I never said we were, you know, like naked!" [He was getting angry.]

"It could have been your wife's back! She could have cut it on the slats."

"That couldn't happen."

"Ok, but what if it did?"

"I don't understand the problem."

[It was time to lay things out.]

"Sex has various facets. It involves touching of course. But it also involves seeing, and even talking. One must display the loved one's body, and your wife must display yours. You must look into her eyes. You must talk to her. You must fight against your own pleasure, concentrate on hers. These and many other practices are necessary, both for pleasure and for satisfaction, and possibly even for love. Go home. Rip away your nightgowns. Keep the lights on. Give it a try, both for your sake and for hers."

[He left the session with uncertainty in his eyes.]

The following week.

"Well?"

"Good Lord! It was really something!" [He was jubilant, as he plopped down into the chair and crossed his legs. He was grinning.]

"You both enjoyed it?"

"Yeah, sure. Oh boy, did we!"

"You looked at each other, and you talked?"

"Yeah, yeah. We did everything!"

"And no embarrassment?"

"Hell, no! We loved the romping and talking! We loved our bodies and the things they could do!"

"And where exactly did you do it?"

"In our daughter's play room. On top of her stuffed animals, surrounded by all her dolls!"

[*Caramba!* I thought once again.]

Retired Rear Admiral John "Cush" Flake was a sixty-two year old white male born into great wealth. He was a tall, thin man, ramrod straight, who entered the office and looked around as if he owned the place. Before I could direct him to the chair, he strode over to it and sat down, then he removed a pipe from his suit jacket, fussed with it for a few moments, then struck a match and puffed away.

"The smoking lamp is not lit, Cush." [I used the Navy jargon and addressed him informally in order to take control of the session, and he slowly removed the pipe from his mouth and covered the bowl with his hand. A few wisps floated up between his fingers.]

"Sorry." [He glared at me, though uncertainly.]

"Time to get down to business. Your intake suggests some sort of language problem?"

"Well yes, and I'm absolutely sure I don't understand it."

"Can you say what it is?"

"Baby talk." [His voice had moved from stridency to a whisper.]

"What about it?

"I can't seem to stop doing it." [Frustration now in his words.]

"Can you give me some examples?"

"I don't wanna do it." [He seemed to be pouting, which was odd given his military carriage.]

"Look here," I said. "This is sex therapy. That's why you've come here. Let's have it!"

"Well, you know, my wife is dead. And mostly I have sexual relations with prostitutes."

"Yeah, so?"

"I say things, you know. To them I mean."

"Attention Admiral!" [He stiffened slightly.] "Let's have it sailor!"

"Well, it's just things. 'Do you like my little pe-pe?' 'Can I touch your cu-cu?' [His voice was now that of a small child.] Just thingies to say."

"This is nonsense," I said. [I wanted to shock him.] "What about your wife? How was that?"

"What do you mean?"

"My God, man! The sex! How was that?"

"Well, there wasn't too much, I guess. Maybe you could say she was cold? Something like that, I mean. Maybe it was me. I don't know."

"You must get a grip, Cush. Seems you're afraid of the body, the way a child might be. You must begin to call it as it is."

"What do you mean, the names? Things like penis and vagina?"

"The words, but not those words, will set you free!"

"What do you mean?" [He was honestly confused.]

"You must call it as it is. 'Do you like my big cock? I like to feel your sweet pussy.' These are not dirty words. They're the appropriate ones. Talk is good. You've already got that. But your words are pushing sex away, rather than engaging in it. The prostitutes will let you say anything. They don't care. But if you get the talk straight, you may find other women. Not prostitutes, but ones you can engage with, and they can engage with you in relationship."

"Okay," he said. "I'll try."

[He cancelled the next three sessions.]

Our second meeting, a month later.

"I've missed you, Cush. What's happening?"

"Sumbitch," he said. "I've been getting more ass than you can imagine! There's pussy everywhere. I get a hard on just thinking about them!"

"Whow, whow! Not in public!" [*Santa Madre de Dios!* I was beginning to realize I'd gone too far, had unlocked a monster.]

"Hell, yes, in public! They all like it, all those beauties! They want cock! Every one of them! And I've got it. Right here!" [He quickly uncrossed his legs and grabbed his crotch. He was grinning.

His tie was waving as he gyrated in the chair, and saliva was running from the corner of his mouth. Delusional, I thought. Quite out of his head.]

"Stop that, Cushie! Right this minute!" [I'd picked up my ruler and was slapping it into my palm, glaring at him in the way of a stern third grade teacher. I'd pushed the button.]

"I sorry," he said. "I a bad, bad boy. I so sorry." [He had slouched down in the chair, released his crotch, and was cringing. Regression to that baby talk, I thought. Then the door opened and the boys in the white coats came in and took him away.]

Madre mia!

Barbra Bogardus was a seventy-five year old mother and grandmother. She was slim and athletic, and had been married to her husband Jimmy for more than fifty years, the two living alone in the farmhouse she had inherited from her father years ago. Dressed modestly in a loose dress that looked to have been fashioned from those flower sacks of old, she stepped gracefully across the floor and settled into the chair across from my desk. In the paper work, she had presented as a "nymphomaniac." Her term. Clinically, that designation is no longer in use.

"I like your hair."

"Oh, thank you!" [My ego overtook my professionalism, momentarily, and for a few seconds it was unclear who was to speak next. Then she did.]

"I'm really here because of my husband."

"What about him?" [Her hair was quite nice too, as was her carefully applied makeup.]

"Well, he's tired. He's getting old. He's almost eighty."

"And?" [She was slow in getting to it.]

"There's only the two of us you know."

"Do you get out and around?" [I was playing her game.]

"Occasionally. Shopping. Things like that."

"And is it women and men, or just one of the two?"

"Oh, no! It's only men."

"Straying?" [As if a tease, but she could see I was serious.]

"No, never! It's only him." [Adamantly.]

"How often?"

"All the time! Everywhere! [She was giving in, letting it out.]

"In the bedroom?"

"Sometimes. But on the floor, the kitchen counter, the bathroom, out in the yard, in the car, we have a comfortable old Buick, up against the wall, dancing naked in the living room and on the couches and chairs in there, just anywhere."

"Under the bed?" [I recalled another case.]

"Of course not! That's silly! How would we move?" [She seemed close to hysteria.]

"And your husband?"

"That's the point! He's getting tired. Maybe sick of it all. I can't tell. I get very excited, you know." [As she was now, though she had slumped down in the chair and was shaking slightly, almost as a child might, this beautiful, dignified woman. *Ayyy pobrecito!* I was feeling her frustration and pain and had to force my professionalism.]

"*Te gusta?* Sorry. I mean, do you enjoy it?" [I knew the answer.]

"No, no! Not a bit! I hate it!"

"And that of course is the problem. Go home. Think about that. What it is that you enjoy. Our time is up. Come back in two weeks.

Two weeks later.

"Good afternoon." [She seemed sure of herself as she moved to the chair and sat down, the box she was carrying resting on her lap. Maybe I had struck the right chord.]

"Hello, hello!" [She was perched at the edge of the seat and was smiling.]

"Relieved?"

"Oh, my, yes!"

"And the sex?"

"Well, my husband is really relieved. Just now and then. And mostly on the bed."

"And do you like it?"

"Somewhat. Now that I've found the real pleasure."

"Which is?"

"This. [She tapped on the box with a finger. I knew what it was. I could smell it.]

"What kind of stuff?" [We were playing the same teasing game as before.]

"Everything! All the time! It's about all I do!"

"Okay. Let's have it, Barbra."

"Here I come!" [She rose to her feet, the box in her hands, and sauntered, hips swinging in a very provocative way, the few feet to my desk. It seemed to take a long time. Her tongue licked her lips in a lascivious manner, as she stared straight into my eyes, and when she reached the desk she handed the box over as if it were herself surrendering.]

"Open it." [She grinned, and I did. And there they were, a baker's dozen, each lovely cupcake frosted in a unique way, and each holding a letter, the thirteen spelling out C-o-n-s-u-e-l-a-L-o-p-e-z. I lifted the C and took a bite. She shivered.]

"My, oh my. This is delicious!"

"I thought you might like it. This is what I do now, all the time." [She slowly pushed her long hair away from her face, and I think she winked.]

"Baking?"

"Oh, yeah! Cake, pies, muffins, brownies and scones, chocolate chippers, sticky buns, and on and on. You name it! And of course cupcakes!" [She was drooling.]

"And you like it?"

"God, yes! I love it! It's so sexy!"

"There you go! It's good to like the things you're doing." [I rose then from my chair and reached across the desk and took her sweaty hand in my own. Our time was up, and I watched her as she sashayed across the room and left me there, smiling.]

So. Three case histories that demonstrate how rich and interesting sex therapy can be. I love my job. And my patients too.

Tonight I'll go out to dinner with Don. He's my best friend. He's a banker, but I don't hold that against him. We'll eat, then go to his house for dessert and brandy. Then we'll talk into the morning's first hours. We might fall asleep, and I might spend the night. There will be no sex.

It's strange I guess. When I was sixteen, wanting to be the Consuela that was hiding inside my Javier, I was obsessed with sex. It didn't matter: trees, mattresses, the bathroom of course, tabletops, in the closet with my mothers fur coat, holding my sister's underwear up to my nose. *Ay, No me gusta!*

It's not that Don is my best friend. Javier would have been all over him. It's the sex itself. After the hormones, the operation, the medicine and the pain as I recovered, slowly becoming Consuela, I began to understand the woman I had become, both in spirit and body. I was a woman whose pleasures are taken in books, music, gardening, and peacefulness. I felt isolated, and I liked that. Sex meant nothing to me, insignificant when placed beside music. Or books, or the many wonders of the world, learned and observed.

And so I am celibate, beyond the usual connotation suggesting denial. I'm simply not interested, and I feel liberated from sex, that known to me through Javier and his grubby passions. There is life after his death, and I set out to take it, in studies, in art and literature, solitude, and in the strange and wonderful worlds presented to me by my patients.

And so it is. *Adios!*

The mad diary of Malcolm Malarkey

Act One

In the Belly of the academy; or,

After Many a semester dies the prof

Mark Axelrod-Sokolov

CHAPTER ONE
Who I am, Why the Fuck Should You Care & Why is this Chapter Title Typed in Courier*?

My name is Malcolm Malarkey. My father was Leopold Bloom. My mother was Molly Bloom. I changed my name from Bloom to Malarkey because Bloom changed his name from Malarkey to Bloom and I didn't want to be associated with my father. Couldn't deal with his slovenliness. His eating with relish the inner organs of beasts and fowls. His keenness for thick giblet soup, nutty gizzards, a stuffed roast heart, liver slices fried with crustcrumbs, fried hencods' roes. Most of all he liked grilled mutton kidneys which gave to his palate a fine tang of faintly scented urine. If the Reader gets the allusion, an "A" for you; if not, read on. Malarkey used to smoke too much, drink too much and fuck too much. Malarkey still doesn't take vitamins, eats dollops of butter, extra slices of bread: three, four, maybe an entire baguette: right, and pisses in public if he has to since it doesn't make any difference anymore. You see, Malarkey suffers from that most fatal of all diseases: birth.

This mad diary begins on Carmel Beach just before sunset. If you can't imagine Carmel Beach just before sunset then google the fucking place. It's one of the most beautiful places on earth and yet, to me, what is this quintessence of dust? Man delights not me; no, nor woman neither, well, maybe not women; though by your smiling, dear Reader, you seem to say so. Imagine that you see Malarkey from behind as he stares out to sea. The shot looks almost like a postcard with Malarkey standing as a lone figure on the deserted white Carmel sands as the sun slowly sets on the horizon. The only sound you can hear is that of the sea breaking onto the shore. Now imagine your eyes as if they were a camera lens that slowly approaches Malarkey and begins to circle him 180 degrees until you see him from the front: his white hair cut closely to the scalp, his white eyebrows, a shaggy white beard; he's dressed somewhat shabbily, carelessly, a faded-green corduroy sport coat with patched elbows, a fading blue work shirt, faded jeans. He's pondering whatever needs to be pondered. More than likely: Weltschmerz, but not necessarily. Weltschmerz can be confused with mere pondering and confusing the two can lead to world woe.

Let's cut from the beach and now imagine the neo-classical Greek pediment of a college building that bears the name etched in peeling plaster: *Citrus City College* with the letters *Cit-Ci* dangling precariously before falling off leaving only the name: *Rusty College*. That's where Malarkey works. It is early September at Citrus City College, and classes have begun a few weeks earlier. Now imagine a panoramic view of a bucolic, Southern California college campus beautifully and meticulously landscaped with dozens of Latino gardeners dressed in Armani suits and ties (furnished by the administration) pruning what always needs constant pruning in order to give students and/or potential parents of potential students the unmitigated perception that the campus is fraught with the diligence of beauty and perfection, a testament to the outrageous tuition that parents of future students or students of the future will have to pay. That is, about $200K for four years of privileged learning.

Imagine too dozens of students mingling on the campus green, tossing Frisbees as others ride penny skateboards in an attempt not to avoid hitting other students oftentimes unsuccessfully;

still other students walk silently from class to class, heads bent, ear buds in place, attending to their mobile phones as they bump into each other, like dodgems, but without the slightest reaction: bump and move on, bump again, move more. Imagine too several professors lying prostrate on the pavement after being nailed by said students on penny skateboard. Some, unconscious, some barely conscious attempting to lift themselves before being pummeled once again by said penny skateboards. Just a sign of the times.

Now imagine a classroom building sign that reads: *Morbittity Hall* named after one of the major college donors, Uriah Morbittity, who made his Orange County millions as an entrepreneur on the cutting edge of automatic urinal flushers (the Uriah Automatic Urinal Flusher) and then imagine that you slowly elevate from the ground floor of that white neo-classical building up to and stop at a second floor window before peering into a class already in session. There you will see Professor Malcolm Malarkey standing, now without a beard, but still dressed somewhat shabbily, carelessly, in a green corduroy sport coat with patched elbows, fading blue work shirt, faded jeans, and a pair of well-worn Boston Celtics' green Converse basketball shoes. Imagine too that Malarkey speaks with a slight Irish accent, that he doesn't suffer fools gladly and, after teaching for decades, that he rarely minces words. As Malarkey turns from a whiteboard to a lectern imagine that Malarkey is clearly agitated.

"Do any of you read? I'm sure you remember the drill. You start from the upper left hand side of the page, move to the upper right hand side of the page. When the line ends skip to the next line and repeat onandonandonandon until the bottom of the page, then turn the page and repeat until there are no more pages to turn unless you're reading Hebrew in which case you'd have to reverse the process. But given the fact few of you can fucking read English the possibility that you can read Hebrew would be out of the question!"
One nineteen-year old student, named Elmo, Malarkey's best student and if one were going to stereotype people could, by appearance and manner alone, be considered as gay, raises his hand in answer to Malarkey's query.

"Thank you, Elmo, I appreciate your help, but it was a rhetorical question."

Elmo smiles and lowers his hand.

"Are you all so fucking lazy that even a novella renders you hapless if not helpless? We're studying *Franny and Zoey* for God's sake, not *Finnegans Wake* or *Giles Goat-Boy*! Salinger couldn't write anything more than Catcher in the fucking Rye and *Franny and Zoey* or that patently stupid "A Perfect Day for Bananafish" whatever the fuck that is, so don't make this superb creation of fiction out to be something more than it is!"

The students are bored, they appear to have heard it all before, and look anywhere, but at Malarkey. Some are enraptured with their cell phones, fondling them, rubbing them against their cheeks, thighs, nuzzling them, gazing wantonly at them as if they were a potential sexual partner; some are texting someone somewhere, perhaps someone in the same classroom with some life-sustaining message about the upcoming festival at Coachella or if they've tweeted recently or have they seen J-Lo was wearing on Instagram and whether there was a side-boob shot or not; one student picks his nose and looks at it as if it were a creature from another planet; another rearranges her halter top making sure her cleavage is appropriately exposed, but no one other than Elmo pays attention to Malarkey. Imagine, too, a muscular young man named Wilson wearing a too-tight, Property of Citrus City College Football t-shirt, leaning back in his desk, arms behind his head flexing his bulging biceps as if in training for Mr. Olympia or attempting to impress the student with the halter top making sure her cleavage is appropriately exposed.

"Why are you even here?" Malarkey asks.

Elmo again raises his hand.

"Thank you, Elmo, once again, it's rhetorical."

Elmo smiles and lowers his hand.

"Don't waste your parents' money. If you don't want to be here, become plumbers, electricians, masons, even pimps, but be bloody good at it!"

Malarkey shakes his head and looks up at the clock which reads 10:50 and at that precise moment, a bell rings.

"Class dismissed, go skateboard or whatever the fuck you do with your lives" Malarkey mumbles to himself.

Malarkey turns back to the white board on which something has been written, but can't quite be made out. He picks up an eraser as if to erase the board as the students file out in relative silence, some stifling a laugh, some making faces at him behind his back, as Too-Tight Wilson cockily approaches Malarkey with a rolled up essay in hand slapping it on his fist almost as if an homage to John Wooden.

"Yo, prof," Wilson begins.

Now Malarkey doesn't acknowledge Wilson immediately, but cringes at the lack of respect. It's another reminder that students are considered "customers" and faculty are "employees" and, as a former dean once admonished Malarkey, "The customer is always right." But it's better than the time a student screamed at him across campus, "Hey, Malarkey, how they hanging!" as he grabbed his genitals. He glances over his shoulder with the slightest smirk on his face since he anticipates what's to follow.

"Yes, Wilson. What can I do for you?"

"I was wondering why I got such a low mark on this paper."

Wilson taps the paper on his fist again.

"Were you now?"

"Yes, I was wondering. Looked good to me."

"Right. Well, let me clarify your wonder, Wilson. Your paper is, well, how can I put it succinctly and in a way a post-Millennial will understand…it's shit. Yes, that's the word…shit. Have I sufficiently satisfied your wonderment?" Malarkey smiles and raises his eyebrows.

"But…"

"There are no buts, Wilson! You don't know the difference between a Pindaric ode and a nematode! Your grammar and syntax are deplorable and your proofreading skills are abysmal! Even your dog wouldn't eat that paper!"

Malarkey smiles and raises his eyebrows once again. Taken aback, his cockiness gone, Wilson storms out of the classroom noticeably angry. Malarkey starts to erase the whiteboard, stops again and looks directly into the eyes of you, the Reader.

"Right. You're probably saying to yourself what a horrible professor. Where's his understanding? His compassion? His interest in his students' welfare? What an unconscionable thing to say. These young adults are the hope of our future, the leaders of tomorrow, the intellects of a brighter Utopia. But that's not the question you should be asking. No, the question you should be asking is this: If you're a parent, you should be asking: What was I doing when my child learned how to be functionally illiterate and academically and socially irresponsible. If you're a student, you should be asking: Since when was there a plague on the art of reading? Milton may have been blind when he wrote, 'A good book is the precious life blood of a master spirit,' but he wasn't demented."

Malarkey raises his eyebrows, shrugs, turns back to the whiteboard to erase it, changes his mind and tosses the eraser on the floor as he leaves. On the white board one reads in bold caps:

"WHAT'S IT GOING TO BE THEN, EH?"

Coda

* The reason the chapter title is typed in Courier New is to let you, the Reader, know that Malarkey is using the painfully old metonymical cliché that by using such a font, which is an old-fashioned typewriter font, it implies he's a writer. Though Malarkey does use a typewriter, he also uses a computer, but since everyone likes to think writers don't use computers, but still use typewriters, Malarkey typed the chapter title in Courier New to lead you to believe that it's the only writerly tool he ever uses. That's bullshit and it will not happen again except in the briefest of circumstances so Malarkey begs for the Reader's indulgence.

CHAPTER TWO
AND HERE'S TO YOU, CHANCELLOR JONES

Imagine now, that you are standing outside the Chancellor's office since Malarkey wasn't going to get away with what transpired in the previous chapter. The nameplate on the door reads: Chancellor J.E. Jones. You enter the office of the Chancellor to discover Malarkey slouching in a chair opposite the 70 something, African-American Jones who's fashionably dressed in what appears to be an Armani suit, white shirt and tie, and black-framed glasses; he's a somewhat robust man, white hair, with a salt-and-pepper beard and speaks in a soothing baritone voice not unlike James Earl Jones.
"Malcolm, you can't say that."

"It's the bloody truth. They don't know a thing."

At that point, Malarkey pretends he's a student and changes the pitch of his voice. "'But Professor Malarkey, why is there so much ironing in Sophocles?' Ironing? In Sophocles? Right, I almost forgot that Sophocles had a dry cleaning business: Alterations by Antigone, Embroidery by Electra, Overlays by Oedipus. What the fuck is that all about!"

"You may know that and I may know that, Malcolm, but there's a right way and a wrong way to go about telling that to students."

"Don't tell me. Was that the wrong way?" Malarkey feigns shock.

"It could be considered micro-aggression," says Jones.

"Wha? Micro-aggression? What the fuck is that? Is that aggression performed under a microscope?"

"No, Malcolm. Malcolm you've got to be more in control of your reactions."

"My reactions."

"Yes, you can go off in a New York second."

"Minute."

"What?" Jones furrows his forehead.

"It's a New York minute. When was the last fucking time you were in New York?"

Jones ignores the question.

"Listen, Malcolm, you're a full professor. You've been teaching for over thirty years, maybe you've lost interest. Maybe the drive is gone. The challenge."

"Or maybe the students just feel entitled. You know how many emails I get from students asking me change their grade for arbitrary reasons! 'But professor, I gave 120%. I read all the books, wrote all the papers, I think I deserve a better grade.' In other words, they did the minimum."

There's a pause in the conversation.

"Have you ever thought about retiring?"

Malarkey ponders the question.

"Oh, right. Retirement. The professorial pasture for all academics who are too old to stud. Have you ever thought about paying me enough to retire on?"

"Yes, well, I understand."

"What do you understand?"

"Yes, I couldn't live on a teacher's salary either, but..."

"But! You gave me a smart two percent rise after over two decades of teaching here. Two-percent! Are you guys in financial crisis? I couldn't buy a year's supply of condoms for that much money. Provided I could use them."

"Well, no, but..."

"But what? Listen, I don't make a half-million dollars a year like you do and second, my ex took half my pension. The day I'll retire is the day they cart me out of here in a pine box. Or has the college downsized to cardboard?"

Jones ignores him.

"What about a sabbatical, Malcolm? Aren't you due for one?"

"Yes. No. I don't know. Maybe. Can't keep track of time. Perhaps my best years are gone. When there was a chance of happiness. But I wouldn't want them back. Not with the fire in me now."

"Then take it."

"I'll think about it. Not sure that's the problem."

"Then what is the problem?"

"The problem is I suffer from chronic irascibility. Do you have a remedy for that?"

"Yes."

"What's that?"

Chancellor Jones remedy to follow.

CHAPTER THREE
FLANN O'BRIEN'S PUB WITHOUT FLANN O'BRIEN

Apparently, the Chancellor answers that question since it's not long after that when Malarkey leaves the Chancellor's office and moseys on down to central Citrus City which is one of the quaintest of quaint towns in Southern California. So quaint, in fact, that it's at the top of Hollywood's list of "Quaintable Towns" and that's why Hollywood often comes to Citrus City in order to film the "Midwest." Like shooting day for night, winter for spring. Hollywood often uses Citrus City to shoot for Bloomington, Indiana or Urbana, Illinois or Iowa City, Iowa or any of a number of Midwestern towns and/or villages in which shooting on site would raise the budget. So, in order to reduce the budget, Citrus City often becomes Bloomington, Indiana or Urbana, Illinois or Iowa City, Iowa or any of a number of Midwestern towns and/or villages.

Citrus City has a lovely roundabout with a small plaza and fountain at its center surrounded by quaint antique stores, quaint restaurants and, of course, a quaint Starbucks on all four corners in case one doesn't want to cross the street in order to buy a $15 Frappuccino Macchiato Latte Espresso with a dollop. Now imagine, a neon sign that flashes, Flann O'Brien's Pub, where, inside, you'll find Malarkey just walking in after having had his little tête-à-tête with Chancellor Jones.

The pub looks exactly like Dublin's "Mulligan's," complete with curved mahogany bar; paneled walls; etc. Malarkey could go into some lengthy description of the place, but that would be a waste of words so just Google Mulligan's and imagine it with the difference being that on the walls are black and white caricatures of Beckett and Joyce, Yeats and Donleavy as well as Flann himself. It's somewhat deserted at that hour since most people aren't drinking at 4.30 as Malarkey walks up to the bar where the thirty-something bartender, Paolo Liliano has his back to him. Malarkey looks puzzled by his presence.

"Where's Seamus?" Malarkey asks with a typical Malarkian attitude.

Paolo turns as he dries off a glass. Paolo has dark features, a square jaw, chiseled chin, an infectious smile. If one were to cast him in a film, one might suggest Rufus Sewell. His temperament is completely the opposite of Malarkey's.

"Seamus isn't here," answers Paolo.

"I may be old, but I'm not bloody blind," Malarkey responds. "If he were here he'd be here, wouldn't he? He'd be standing right where you're standing, drying off the same fucking glass you're drying off. But I didn't ask you that, did I? I asked you where he was."

"He took another job."

"Where?"

"Kansas. Topeka."

"Why the fuck would he go there? Who goes to Kansas? Jayhawks don't exist. You know what a fucking Jayhawk is?"

"No, not a clue."

"Jayhawks were guerrilla fighters who battled with pro-slavery groups from Missouri. Why the fuck Kansans would invent a bird to represent guerrilla fighters is beyond me."

"Me too."

"So, why'd he go to Kansas?"

"Death in the family."

That statement gives Malarkey pause. Death usually gives one pause whether it's one's own or someone else's so he changes the course of the conversation.

"Right. So, who the hell are you?"

"I'm Paolo Liliano. And who the hell are you?" Paolo holds out his hand, but Malarkey doesn't shake it.

"I'm Malcolm Malarkey and I came in here to get a stinkin' drink. What's it to you, polo?"

"Paolo."

"Whatever. What's a fucking Italian doing bartending in an Irish pub anyway?"

Paolo stops wiping the glass and leans over the bar.

"All the Irish bartenders were too drunk to work. So, what'll you have, Malcolm?"

"That's Professor Malarkey to you."

"Okay, Professor Malarkey what'll you have?"

"My guess is you don't know shit about drink making, do you?"

"Try me."

"Okay, gimme a Black Nail."

Paolo finishes drying a glass.

"Bushmills and herbal Irish Mist. You want it with or without the orange peel or would you prefer orange bitters?"

Malarkey's eyes get wide.

"Surprise me," he snidely answers.

What the Reader will eventually discover is that Paolo is not merely the bartender, but the new owner. Other things about Paolo will also become apparent. Now you've got to imagine it's a few hours later in the day. As a matter of fact, there's a Guinness Bottle Draught Wall Clock that reads: 7.30 so if the Reader is adept at reading then s/he knows he's been there for three hours. Malarkey sits in a booth by himself, nursing yet another Black Nail when a tall, leggy, twenty-something blond wearing excessively short cut-offs saunters up to his booth. She cocks her head to one side as if trying to think who

Malarkey is and points a finger at him. Malarkey, in his usual Black Nail stupor, doesn't give her much attention.

"I know you," she says. "You're Doctor Malarkey, aren't you?"

Malarkey looks up and squints.

"Yes, but only during urgent care hours."

"My name is Tiffany, Tiffany Tustin. I went to high school with your daughter, Andrea."

Malarkey smiles and nods politely, but he's clearly not interested in carrying on any conversation that could, potentially, lead him into a dalliance with one of his daughter's friends which could then lead to a possible affair which could then lead to a possible video which could then lead to the video going viral which could then lead to it being viewed on Facebook or YouTube or any other social media outlet in the fucking universe which could then lead to another meeting with Chancellor Jones which would probably lead to his dismissal. After all, he's not Donald Trump and doesn't think about shtupping his daughter or her friends.

"Come here often?" Tiffany Tustin asks seductively, leaning across the table, exposing her abundant cleavage and smiling a seductive smile.

"Maybe too often."

"Could I buy you a drink?" Tiffany Tustin asks seductively.

"Maybe...when you're older," he answers with a smile and raised eyebrows.

"Too much for you to handle, eh?" Tiffany Tustin asks seductively.

"Not without outside resources," Malarkey answers with a smile and raised eyebrows.

"Are you afraid of me?" Tiffany Tustin asks seductively.

"No, I think you're the most attractive of all my daughter's friends," Malarkey answers with a smile and raised eyebrows.

Tiffany Tustin gets a very quizzical look on her face. She obviously doesn't get Malarkey's allusion.

"Huh?"

"Mais ou sont les nieges d'autun," Malarkey answers with a smile and raised eyebrows.

"Sorry?"

"That's French for 'have a good night.'"

Tiffany Tustin shrugs her shoulders.

"Nice seeing you again, Doctor Malarkey. Say hello to Andrea for me." And Tiffany Tustin sashays away, her butt cheeks casually creeping beneath the fringes of her cutoff denims.

"Mon plaisir," Malarkey answers and raises his glass.

Paolo has been listening to the exchange as have three other men sitting at the bar who look a lot like Beckett and Joyce and Yeats all of whom stare at Malarkey wondering what he was thinking.

By now, the Guinness Bottle Draught Wall Clock reads 9.30 and Paolo is sitting with Malarkey in the same booth that Tiffany Tustin had tried to seduce him in. Paolo is sober; Malarkey not so much and he tends to slur his words as he nurses a Guinness Bitter.

"My cousin moved to Philly from Arona about fifteen years ago. I came soon after," Paolo says.

"Didn't W.C. Fields say he'd rather be buried than be in Philly?"

"No, I think he said he preferred Philly to being buried."

"Same thing. Where's Aroma? It doesn't sound Italian."

"Arona, not aroma."

"Whatever."

"Outside Milan. On Lago Maggiore."

"I don't know one fucking lake from another over there. Are you mafioso?"

"Not anymore," Paolo smiles as if there might be some truth to it. "I left that to my father."

"So, you gave up the mafia life to become a bartender? It's a bit of a step down, isn't it?"

"No, I gave it up to be a father."

"Where's the mother? Having it off with Berlusconi?"

"No, she died of breast cancer."

Malarkey is pained by that. Malarkey is often pained by those sorts of things since Malarkey's mouth often works faster than his brain.

"Oh, fuck, Malarkey. Sorry...I'm..."

"How would you have known?"

"Sometimes my mouth works faster than my brain. It's a disease. Too many black mails."

"Nails."

"That's what I said."

Malarkey takes another sip of Guinness.

"Listen, I think you've had enough. You need a ride home?"

"No, I have my bike."

"Does it have a seat belt?"

Malarkey pauses as if pondering the question.

"Uh, no, maybe."

"Then you need a ride home. I'll bring your bike inside."

And so he does. Brings Malarkey's bike into the bar before escorting him to the parking lot and gently tucking him into the passenger seat before he gently secured a seat belt around him.

"So, where do you live?"

"Live?

"Yes. Where do you reside? Lounge? Eat? Sleep? That sort of thing."

"Around the corner and down the block, over the river and through the woods, to grandmother's house we go; the horse knows the way to carry the sleigh, through the white and drifted snow!"

And so Paolo attempts to take Malarkey home.

(4109)

Audience

(from *Play, A Novel*)

Alan Singer

Act I, Scene 6: A lofty turret room of the renegade Gonzogo's castle. Stone walls, streaked with a furry dampness. Instruments of torture: a rack, pulleys, hooks.
Gonzogo is cinching Rosalinda's wrists to the rack. She barely resists.

GONZOGO: Look upon these remnants of previous leather bindings. Are they not curled against the dowels like perched birds who never flew again from these bare lime twigs?

ROSALINDA: My limbs will not survive the test. Why not cut out my tongue to soothe your wrath, since it will warble the notes of my innocence forever in your hearing?

GONZOGO: That tongue I should have cuddled with my lips? It would have been my pleasure to make it my pet, were it not such a cur to the truth.

ROSALINDA: Signore, my only falsity was the truth of my love for Fernando, whose bones your axe set to as if you were a chopper of wood. So, you watered the tree of your hatred with his blood. We did see how it rose to the knees of your breeches, you waded so deep.

GONZOGO: I will go deeper yet.

ROSALINDA: In me, with your roughest blade. Be quick!

Gonzogo reaches for the dagger in his belt.

ROSALINDA: But stay. Do you not wish to know what it would have been like, had I parted my lips for you? Thusly, at least you might know what you have slain.

GONZOGO: What? Give me reason to do honorably that which would have otherwise have seemed dishonor? Defile a slut? By your leave mistress, I will.

Gonzogo wrenches Rosalinda's mouth toward his own by the scruff of her neck. When he crushes his mouth upon hers, Gonzogo gives out an agonized shriek and falters backwards to the floor. Rosalinda cries out. She bares her incarnadine teeth. The tip of a sewing needle glints minutely in their bloody grip. She spits.

ROSALINDA: Quicker am I to the scabbard of my tongue than you to the scabbard on your belt Signior. To be plain, the point of my blade was already unsheathed in my words-- which you mistook for the weakest flesh—and already tipped with the adder's bile. The bite at the other end of the needle was easy enough to bear, knowing how my taunting tongue, skewered on the very shaft of the needle, would bid you good death.

 Marry, my tongue bleeds from the wound that wombed the needle's sting. I would not deny it. Unlike yourself, I do bleed the evidence of a murder.

 But you Signore, you are dead.

"Yes. The piece has a working title. *Killer Killing Killers.* Many scenes, but all superficially disarticulated from one another. Except of course that they are all scenes of murder. One after another. Murder keeps them interested."

How many times have I begun the conversation with my potential backers this way?

As with my surgeon, we meet in restaurants. Or in the bars that are ante-rooms to restaurants, pretexts for eating. For acting. It is an act of devotion, if I can conjure the funds from their hip pockets.

My potential backers wish to divine the meaning of their investment. It is my job to make them believers, in the very manner of the original mystery players. The devil could bare his backside on stage and no one laughed at the shagginess of the hair that whipped the swagger of that dark orifice. Well, I want them to take it on faith that their money is already a token of sacred knowledge, which no accountant could ever divulge for them. They require instead the offices of a priest of dramaturgy.

Is it not art, after all, that we are discussing, glasses in hand, our mouths quite full?

"Think of *yourself* as the meaning of the play," I tell them. "Do you not recognize your special sensitivity to the human condition?" Then I delve into the body cavity, stroking the choicest organs. The stomach, the heart. I conjure a plot, a fate. I make a character stoop. I unfold a fabric of suffering, spread it out before them.

"The production is a sort of tablecloth upon which we will break bread. Such knowledge of the human heart we will purvey." I inspire them to appreciate our partnership. "You in your capacity as a producer, me in my capacity as a producer of miracles."

So, I inveigle them, knowing how insatiable the hunger for the right feeling can be. Touching human organs is a tricky business. Not to say "sticky." Well, you want to breathe life into the idea of the play. You want them to feel the fragility, the shortness of that breath. And you want them to stomach it when you suck that breath away. But be chary of the heartstring strung too tightly. Don't snap the bond by suturing things up too tightly. Well, I sound like a medical man myself. Not surprisingly.

Believe me, I have spent my hours on the table, dying to be the surgeon, not the rattling patient. Dying, if truth be told.

It can indeed be told.

******

Dr. Todorow stirred in his seat, in the fifth row, center of the *Crooked Hat Theater*, observing my high stepping entrance from stage left, though the stage set, a curved wall of mirrors, reversed that direction for the audience, held briefly as they might have been, in the grip of illusion. Not least the illusion that here was a healthy specimen of an actor.

No such illusion would have sway over the un-confoundable heart carver. As he tells it, he was already prickly with the foreknowledge that constantly hums in the fingertips of a man whose senses teeter against unpredictable densities of tissue as they yield to the sheerness of whetted steel. Such is the surgeon's preternatural attunement to what is next. We all squirm in our balcony seats with the tickle of such anticipation in our tails. Who can help it? Well, we are not doctors after all. We cannot help.

As I set my silent, tip toeing foot to the floor behind Siegfried The Magician's wand waving figure, the garrote dangling from my fingertips like a shimmering necklace, my entire physique shuddered with the first fist-thumping blows of the heart muscle that suddenly lurched within my breast. The even more massive thump of my entire body upon the floorboards of the stage, as tremorous as a sandbag plunging from the lighting grid above our heads, caused Siegfried The Magician, meant as he was to be caught unawares by the garrote that was already skittering across the stage, to flinch and cower. Precisely the response that my character's exaggerated light-footedness was intended to forestall. The director should have halted the production.

But the unsubtle foot was now stomping its way from my chest to my shoulder and down my arm, finding its mark, so that the recognition scene of a drama all too horribly recognizable to me, might unfold to its fatal conclusion.

Luckily, luckily I had a secret collaborator in the drama that I could not have authored by myself. Dr. Todorow's rush to the stage outpaced the giant foot trodding upon the life that I now imagined to be a mouse scurrying frantically to escape the enclosure of my narrowing chest. He found me athwart the mark where the stage action was meant to have progressed, my eyes spread wide and overflowing with the light that showered from the pole-grid above our heads, my arms and legs flung away, the body trying to save itself by reckless abandonment of the convulsing torso.

He knew what to do. He seized the mouse tail. With my pulse still throbbing in his thumb he raised himself on one knee under the wash of a particularly glaring spotlight that must have made the squinting spectators wonder if this wasn't a continuation of the drama they were so engrossed in. Passing his open hand across the face of the audience, as if to wipe away the greasy film on a window, he ordered the auditorium to be cleared. The ambulance might have disgorged from his mouth it appeared with such instantaneity.

The siren of the ambulance, hovering over my lurching stretcher as we raced out of the bleak tunnel of my breast-beating terror into the salvific illumination of the operating theater, still rings in the tunnels of my hearing. Someone was holding my hand, leading me, though I was not following on my own legs. Voices spoke as if I were their echo chamber. They did not speak to me. I was scissored free of my clothes. I was shifted from gurney to table. A heavy glove was laid upon my mouth. I breathed it in as I was instructed. I felt vague fingers snuggling in my nostrils, in my throat.

As the fur grew thicker in my consciousness I was nonetheless aware that another stage was awaiting my appearance. Dr. Todorow's eyes beamed the key-light that, I chillingly recalled, only the risen dead can give report of. My complete loss of consciousness at that moment did not dim the scene of action that was about to transpire, though I was no audience for it. They discovered my heart.

I'm making an inference. I am, after all, alive.

*****

An inference, fittingly enough, is what I ask of my potential backers, I don't deny it. For them it might be characterized as the leap of faith that one hopes will be fortuitously winged with success. I am the one, am I not, promising to make those wings sprout.

I felt the nibs of those wings scratching my throat while

we waited for the first drinks to arrive. The bardic genius who first dipped his quill into the inkpot was at the feathered end of the bargain. So, I must flock to answer their questions. I am, after all, one of a company.

"Yes, the piece has a working title. *Killer Killing Killers.* You can take it either way. Either the killer is adjectivally motivated, a killing kind of killer. Or have it otherwise. The killer kills. Of course, if you try to go one way, the other will follow."

My potential backers are of the world that knows the difference between an adjective and a noun. They aren't cunts, as our Pinter would have his character say it. I have taken part in his audiences, at the more fashionable theatrical houses, no doubt among the ilk of the very backers who sat before me now. They sport turtle-neck sweaters, cashmere scarves, ascots. Not cowboy hats and string ties. They speak languages that did not mother them. They have traveled. They have eaten exotic meats. They have attained their full stature as men, and the occasional startlingly attractive woman. Their photographs, among the faces of other directors and playwrights and actors, stare out at us from the walls of even such restaurants as this, where I invite my potential backers to swirl the wine in the glass, to lean back against padded leather and entertain my proposal. The drinks had arrived.

"But don't get the wrong idea. There is humor. The humor, you see, is in the blood. Think of the old humours of the blood that would have bubbled in the bard's time and you're on your way to the insight that is my tickling inspiration. I seem to give you only violence in my play. Seemingly discrete scenes, like blood-soaked breadcrumbs, dropped without a pathway to remember. But my audience will pick them up. They will see the humor of it in the end because they will have no choice.

"I've been accused by my critics of worse convolutions, believe me.

"So, yes the play is one scene after another, you understand, of killing. But one thing after another implies history, doesn't it? The meaning will of course be recognizable to my audience by cues of costuming and scenery, if not by the distinct idioms echoing our hoary theatrical past. Each scene will be dressed out in the costuming and language of our Greeks, our Jacobeans, our Victorians, our Moderns the whole playlist of our great masters. The dignity of the theater itself is to be honored in these scenes, despite the rampant gore.

"So, at least seemingly it will be only one scene after another of the knife piercing the eye, the garrote nearly severing the vertebrae (there are tricks to this trade), the gunshot smoldering in the chest, the poniard twisting in the groin, the anal penetrations with the fire-dripping iron poker (tricks, as I say). But *seemingly* is the point.

"Because you haven't heard the best part. You haven't really understood what it is I am proposing yet. And that is as it should be. Your suspense is the audience's suspense. You will know what they will know, unexpectedly, as it happens in the most realistic life. I am such a mimetic artist you see, quite contrary to the label "experimentalist" which my critics have stitched upon the fabric of my career and which, like all the white-coated labroratorists who so dutifully attend to our mortality, simply frightens the audience away. Some call them doctors.

"I tear that label out of the lining of every performance.

"Well, here is the proof of my plot-making proficiency. One scene after another of killing etc. One scene after another of the knife piercing the eye etc. Oh, they'll get the gore, our audience. They may even be briefly startled by their capacity for boredom, the edge of their seats pricklingly numbing the backs of their legs. They'll get the gore. But they'll have missed the point of the poniard, if you catch the flourish of its twinkling in my eye. Until they have seen enough, until they have seen past the costuming, even past the face paint.

"'But he is already dead,' they will now mutter to themselves. One killer killed by the next in scene after scene. Such is the appearance they will have been given by us jointly, should you take my hand in this venture. Now they will feel the confidence of their smug judgment in the smile-primped corners of their lasciviously rouged mouths. Men are plumped with as much blood as women in the snide curling of their lips that accompanies the presumption to criticize.

"For the killer has, with each killing, taken a bow of sorts, slowly and deliberately turned full face toward the witnessing audience—releasing the weapon of choice to the incriminating clatter of the stage floor—before abruptly making his exit from the scene.

Until the next scene, when the actor's face will be recollected more sharply.

"So now they will be embarrassed for the actor, more so for the writer and for the producer whom they will believe have let the theatrical sleight slip from the hand.

"'The same actor,' they will whisper to one another in the thickening murk of their seats. They are having to use the same actor. How are we meant to believe in these characters?"

They won't know how they were meant to mouth these criticisms until the actor speaks for herself.

"In the final scene she addresses herself directly to the audience. When her face turns over her shoulder, they feel the massive liquid queasiness of the passengers in a lifeboat lifted by a sudden swell rolling off the back of a whale. So, the memory comes to each member of the audience. In every one of the preceding scenes the killer has curiously paused, just so. Before taking the first steps towards his hasty escape, he has paused. He has turned his face to the audience in exactly this way, as if he had something to say. Then thinking better, tucking the quick tongue of himself into the folds of silencing darkness that close behind him at the back of the stage, he is gone.

"But this time, after so many scenes of carnage, he speaks. She speaks.

'I've been watching you. How did you not notice? I, I am always the killer'. What the audience thought they had unmasked as the disqualifying artifice of the performance, was, of course, the point of the performance.

"Well, this reversal of roles is what I am thinking of now. For the ending. Not bad, I admit. But much can change in the course of rehearsals and rewritings, the accidents of time that stretch before us to opening night. The final ending will come later. You must permit yourselves the suspense. What's a plot without a reversal of fate?"

Final Scene: Subject to Revision
A butcher shop. White tile walls. A high counter with a broad view of displayed meats.
Before the counter, Smartson is just leaving the stage, stepping over

the hacked corpse of his wife Sofia, his grip yet unrelenting upon the axe-handle. The axe-head bobs drippingly over his left shoulder.

SMARTSON: *He stares with a new and frenzied concentration over his right shoulder at the audience. Here commences a monologue.* I've been watching you. How did you not notice? I, I am always the killer.

      You've seen me perhaps. But you haven't noticed.

      And if you are keener of eye than I imagine, you knew I was always the killer in every scene, whatever the scene, whatever costume I colored it with. I was always the purveyor of this eye [winks at audience], tossed over my shoulder like a coin to sop you, to distract you, as I spirited myself from the stage. Always the same ending. At the terminus of each scene you know what to expect, so far…as far as you know anyway.

      If you have the keener eye, you were not fooled by the appearance that I was always killed in the subsequent scene, an actor dressed like me, spoken like me, my name his again. If you have the keener eye, hungry for notice of your own, you might say, under your breath, mildly, laughingly to your seat-mate, *it is the same actor killing again.*

      But still, you've missed a thing or two.

      You thought that I, a man murderer, was a man.

Turning ever more frontally to the audience, unbuttoning the all too conspicuous fly of her pin-striped trousers, and with the violent affection of a mother plucking her toddler's arm from the curb, she releases a springy rubber phallus from the flapping vent.
Then, emitting the shriek of a woman who has just stepped over a mouse, she rips open the black velour-trimmed tuxedo vest-- fastened from first button to last under the suit jacket--watch fob flying, and looses one alabaster bosom from the false shirt-front now crumpled around her neck. The rosy nipple is pertly erect under her provocative fingertip, proving its authenticity, at least to the first three rows.
BLACKOUT

4 Poems

Fanny Howe

Before Forever Lost

Many mothers I knew
Walked the underworld
To find their children
Sleeping under a ramp.
Canals and cans, urinals and sandals
Broken boys & girls
With rings still sore in their skin.
Mothers wept away the hours
While the starlight combed our hair
Under windows cresting overhead.
Mothers carried in their pockets,
Ear buds, candy bars and bread.

The mother of the gutter suggested:

Go build an altar, kids.
Not just a stage but with all of you
Eating and playing
Airplanes and dolls, margarine
From toast on your hands.
Why are you crying?
Let's shake up a rhythm
To match the rain on asphalt.
Lips in our teeth to shut
Our sorrow.

Get up, get up!

Up stood a child, dirty and loud, and her boots furry.
An immigrant from the United States.

She went everywhere with me, this disgrace with no money.

She had the pallor of—say
Someone who never passed through the God phase.

Silvery gray is its weather.

Soft char rubbed off a gun barrel or an eyelid.
She didn't want others to see the way she saw herself.

My second without a first.
Eyes that follow me

From plain to plane
Over the sea and far away—
Through the debris of former species.

Who are you to stay so relative:
Are we two, one, or past?

Are? Were, will be.

Cant

Peter Hughes

1

One of the deepest stations of the Metro - or a Metro - maybe Rome, perhaps Berlin. It might have been in Paris. Toledo in Naples? Some nights I think it could have been in the Diros caves, or on a waterway deep within the limestone halls of Derbyshire. In one of these locations, or perhaps another, I had an idea. I wrote it in a notebook which I carried in a canvas bag. Later that evening, as I left some unremembered bar, I realised that I no longer had the bag. I hope to replace it over the next few days.

2

Life without the bag drags on. Without the notebook I have been unable to continue my projects and am scribbling on the back of an old job application. It was mixed up with drafts of poems and a take-away menu for a place I don't remember and have almost certainly never been to. The job application came to nothing. After lunch I had a dream in which people were arguing about which metro system had the shallowest station. One guy proposed an example with a man-made roof. Marie said it really shouldn't count unless it went properly underground.

3

I've acquired another bag, from a charity shop. It has an adjustable strap and smells of tobacco and mints. The adjustable strap keeps slipping back to where it had been. Perhaps that's why it was in the charity shop. That and the smell of tobacco. It smells like down the back of a sofa. I'd like to smoke, just the one. Maybe one a month. I'd hide them in a place I can't remember, or in my bag. I'd put it down again in places where I used to go. You kick the habit of belonging early, can't start again.

4

The contents of the lost notebook are forgotten and putting on weight. There was probably an amazing poem very near the front, where the enthusiasm of starting a new notebook is at its most intense. Just after the best bits from the previous notebook have been copied into the new one. That opening section which makes the quality of the writing promise more than it can ever deliver. Still all written neatly in the same pen. The poem was probably clever but also full of feeling, riding its tightrope, illuminated, glittering. An invisible audience is looking up in awe, breathless.

5

An imaginary audience up to its elbows in sticky popcorn. You smell of candy floss. Of course it might have been a clown car, maybe overtaken by the stunning rider on the magnificent horse. Cymbal crash. A tall white horse without a saddle. Without a rider. Without a horse. The feeling that after you'd stopped smoking all the tiny lights and disembodied glows, the featherweights of earth and ritual sacrifice just vanished from the world and left the sky and art a little colder. The blue lighter, translucent and almost empty, kept in the side pocket of the lost bag.

6

I imagine all the other days the bag contained. Microscopic traces in the weave of the canvas. Archaeological airs. The places where I didn't want to stay but still can't do without. One of the few things left on the phone is an early Eric Truffaz piece, hi Eric, and the drumming is amazing. Not that the trumpet isn't. But, you know, sometimes the drummer needs some credit. Marc Erbetta. Complimenti. I reach into the absent bag for the notebook. Drumming gives you something to do with your hands, and your feet. It's usually too late to take up drumming.

7

After a tricky afternoon I woke up as it darkened and thought I'd better go out before it got too late. Maybe a pint of Abbot in the pub by the park. The best part of a second passed before I realised that I didn't live in that town any more. Are forgetting where you live and forgetting your bag in the underground connected? It's good to have contact details on the first page of the notebook. This may be helpful if you lose it but it is mainly useful if you forget where you live and who you are.

8

I once rushed home to let the dog out, stopped as if falling over a cliff in my head, then remembered the dog had died eight years before. Writing is important but there's only so much of the world you can contain in the kind of notebook that fits into the kind of bag you can lose on the underground. She went twice around the block and I headed north. I never really found my feet again but I did learn to tread water. You can see the bright lights of the hospital from the far side of the valley.

9

There was a downstairs bar in the main street of my home town. There was often live music. A selection of singer-songwriters, some local, some itinerant. Dimly lit and ill equipped acoustically and with regard to beer. It was all corners where parts of me still sit bathed in a solution of feedback and minor chords, plectrum clicks, the distinctive zip of fingertip callous on medium gauge bronze wound strings. Never figured out the best way to remove the pegs to change the strings. Sit in. The satisfaction of a firm capo. So many cover versions and different keys.

10

Overcrowded, unpredictable trains with different absent owners. People bang in UKIP signs, their distinctive rhubarb and custard colouring fading to grey in vacant front gardens. Custodians squint down the road at dusk, scowling at any signs of life. Behind the playing field, someone dives under a train. Later the train reverses back to Cambridge. Reach for a mint. Sweeten the breath, rot the teeth still further. In long-exposure photographs of the era the presence of any individual becomes invisible, or reduced to vapour trails and ghostly whispers. A plane up in the last light takes a mother into exile.

8 Poems

Meredith Quartermain

LOST DOG EAST-END BLUES DETOUR

Do you have a points card?
Can it make a sandwich?
Why wait till January?
Did you know it's free?

Do you know the time?
Would you enjoy it?
When does it leave?
Are you driving?

Are you missing parts of words?
Parts of January?
Parts of free?

Are you working for nature?
Do you need one?

Can you break down

January
free
sandwiches?
How far did you go?

Are you done
with missing parts?
Did you wash them?

Are you sure they're free?
Not sandwich?
Not nature?
Did you call the movie?
How long?

Whaddaya mean – read?
Is it nonGMO?
What market?
Are you checking in?

CAMERA W0MAN

on location filming
waste connections
they lie together
rustle of this and that
their work done

their roots sprung
from completed forms
of fur bearing animal
ally oop shirt you try
to keep on walking
the yo yo
twenty bucks

I got shoes and shit too
log in to my private pump
king fitness class
steel balls on loop-the-lope
while they get this
fun-raising shot
in the fire alarm
full time airlocker

waffles yes waffles
are courteous to
neighbours' snakes
keep the garden
rolling
cut
action
hands up SFPD car
top stripe pe-ony pe-ople
flasher lightly sneaking
past boom clapper dolly

gimme the juice, make it chopper, over
I'll copy that over apple Winnebago

video replay over distant auto-lock
fiddle over police roars
over still rolling over

they get worse too
but she doesn't feel like him

NOVEMBER 6

tell me about habit, stop sign
lest we forget

Baldwin: the role you play
becomes trap

girl walking one foot ahead of the other
step only on this crack
only this one

mother striding through school yard
worried angry

the fading leaves
flesh gone to lace

cluster in last heaps
of clasped hands
memories

knotted habits
the breakfast cereal
the bed time
the shirt colour
all the architecture you build

just thoughts I think I'm in hell
therefore I am: Rimbaud

no entry except lymphocytes

ZERO INFINITY

kick it up two three four
kick it up babes
supporting babes
caves supporting slaves

this area is a a a
arena rezonery
cover with water

wave to the panda
caution empire tape
made in USA

they reported to office
hopefully they'll sprout
candidas

they soap box well
they asked their advice
having a a a avenue

if they're running today
there's more money
and they gotta wireless
and they gotta highway

VIADUCT

before you act
the idea of the act
you voyage out
you think
somewhere you
already there
already your selfie
shadow ahead
your outline on pavement
foreshadow further
and further out
of whack
not there you
box work
for in whack
submergency
outline puddle
mirror

spaceships crash other spaceships
drag wreckage build more
video screen control panel
shadow pavement

ROPETURE

man roped to shopping cart
his lean bare torso
pulls mountain
of sacks of pop tins
parachute yank backward

rope to hang
French rupe skirt
no, it's jupe
rupe is nothing
unless rupture

rope around science
museum railing
ties rafted bundle
of sailboats

knotted nylon line
not rope
line is longer
yarn to pleasure craft
in the sci-lence
with the rote

WITHSTAND THE BLOW

hug the wind
the stucco caressing creeper
Millross Avenue undertow
of automated looms
bulrushes and catkins
meow
the great love
every minute
walking alongside
reading me reading
he each kiss of
our two lives
loves

AUTONOMY AT THE ABYSS

he hated his name but of course
he had to be called that
his father had been Autonomy
and his father before that
and his great grandfather
before

5 Poems

Jake Marmer

Not-Here / Not-Now

"Remaining here-and-now, the world begins to lure us with a feeling, an intuition, of what the poet Robert Kelly speaks of as the not-here/not-now."

- Jerome Rothenberg, "Poetics of the Sacred"

in the room with rolled up carpets
in the room of reversed roles
in the empty room

in the room with a bulging
window sill. in the room over-
hanging a cliff. in the cliffnotes of a room

in the duly noted room
in the room where nobody coughs

in the room where interruptions
have no name
in a room named
after an interruption

in the room that's tantamount
in the room where one time
in the never before room

in the room where it all
happened. in the room
where all that happened is stored
in the storage room

Four Questions: A Study

> Questions exist as a way of saying
> There is no opposite to what I'm thinking
>
> - Bernadette Mayer

#1

further question as in "are there any further questions" which is a question that does not invite or validate it merely points to the physical location that is outside of the now, is further, is off the course, is fucked up, is the most difficult question to answer with the question even though it would seem that that's precisely its purpose –

it is nearly impossible to question it without betraying your location on the map of exile from answers

#2

"wouldn't you rather" question that opens up the door to much worse things that could be happening to you this moment, and is one of the many instances when verbiage asserts a feasible reality or expands what you know by taking away the floor, music, speech as it nails itself to a rhetorical doorpost and you feel lucky to be holding on to the handle that this question is

#3

if you were stuck on the desert island question which is a lot like the question that opens up a realm of possibility of much worse things that could be happening – but more so –this is the older, more assimilated cousin, and I am afraid of its beardless finality, the implicit abandonment, the hell of being left on that island with your just one record or screwdriver or the book you start hating the minute you nominate it because it is now your Chosen Book, and I don't understand the claustrophobia of this moment, isn't it just another way of asking you to name things you can't live without, I want to understand why this feels different

#4

the sort of a why-not question, which constitutes no more than 0.2% of all why-nots, and is smothered in the pillow of your autobiography and is the other side of the word "dream"– this question is called the true candle it is called the scholar's joke and it is not the question that gets asked because it does not have a duration it is a lot like passing from one room into the next but first of the two rooms had already disappeared

Please Don't Panic at the Disco

please don't panic at the disco
I will, I will panic at the disco

please don't panic at the wig styling contest
I'm going to run outta that contest with my wig tips flailing in the air

please, PLEASE, stay cool at the cellophane philosophy lecture
I'm going to lose my shit three seconds into that lecture

please don't panic at the bris
…

please don't panic in the middle of a religious experience
no panic – no transcendence

if I am not for my panic, who am I?

please don't panic at the deportation picnic
I might choke on my refugee accent all over your picnic tables

you're panicking inside my misplaced meta-confectionary poem
THE VOICE OF THE AUTHOR SAYS I FOUND THE SOURCE OF
MY PANIC AND WILL NOW REMAIN CALM AS A JERUSALEM
CIGARETTE BUTT IN THE WRONG WALL AT THE WRONG TIME

please don't panic at the disco
     I am the panic at your disco
     you're drawing a closed door in the middle of the sky and
     anthropomorphizing it too
     can't put a cactus up someone's rump to get them dancing
     I'm your alien panic with nowhere to go so I'll crawl inside your
     pop song and sing
          my heart out

Lake/Robinson Duo

> *...in black and in back it's roses and fostered nail*
> *-Clark Coolidge*, Blues for Alice

discursive owlish power
dispersement & likeable straw
strata beads
face otherwise
Beatrice and flat deaf-mirrors
stream of craft, hoarse
cough, net solved, metered
truck discusses fitting well
near the music school

boudoirs full of Folger's where
debased bunkers revealing it
pants draft raft posterity
window why not why graft
flippant panting pundit
between us zebra-drag
vibraphone calling wall a wall
brevity whittled flattening the rest
gusty stepping out light's side
ways where hotly scissors
rabbit hat violin-mind nothing
visible bird peak post roast
modern tag bristles/brush

Oliver Lake (horns) / Don Robinson (drums)
San Francisco, July 2016

This Poem Needs a Title

*Based on an improvisations at the Jewish
Community Library, Oct 2015 with John Schott
and Ben Goldberg and at Kehillah Jewish High
School with Stu Brotman in Mar 2016*

I'd like to end this set with the newest poem
        so new it hasn't been written yet
though I don't want to give it away   then
again it won't get written so there's nothing to
give away   the piece is called "This Poem
Needs a Title" which is both a title and the
sentiment   "sound and sentiment"
        though it's not very sound-centric but
then again it could've been called   "Four
Questions" or "Not-Here/Not-Now" – but here
instead of entitlement you have desire, no –
        a need and not the poet's need   but
the need of the poem itself

any poem I guess is a squeezed need   a lever
pushing some fruit or another   the juice is
pouring down into reader's mouth   but
what if it's scarier than that   what if the
poet already squeezed the fruit at home in his
loneliness and drank the juice and the audience
gets   the pith   a pithy poem
        you can hypothesize   you can write
an essay   the whole class is writing essays
about the taste lurking inside the pith   and
the question is   how do you squeeze the
juice   in performance, off the page   while
on the page?   how do you stop yourself from
touching the fruit?

of course the poem itself doesn't "need"   I'm
not into spooky post-modern pseudokabbalistic

hoohaa   though some of my best friends
are   poem as a breathing thing, text-is-alive
nonsense   it would be pretty great
        but of course I'm here to dispel that myth
because it's the poet that needs a title   what
kind of a title?   "Mr." or "Dr." are both good
and distinguished titles   or there's Junior
which is terrible   like, there's Allen
Ginsberg's "Song" but this is "Song, Jr."

        of course "poet" is a title   "my husband
is a poet"   it's more like "my husband needs a
title" or rather "my poem needs a wife" – isn't
poem's relationship to its title a bit spousal?

I'm not married to "This Poem Needs a Title" title
        I can and should change it   in fact
search for the title is the message of the title –
right? a title   if anything it's like a
classified ad – a spontaneous rambling poem less
than 10 minutes in the making but an old soul, all
about itself, a public servant, looking for a
perfect companion, who enjoys dissonant music,
mirrors – join me for – for what?   willing to
travel

speaking of travel   I originally wrote this
poem in the car driving to Santa Cruz on
Highway 17   this massive thing of constant
veering   I couldn't stop to type
        though isn't poetry both drunk-driving
and texting at once   a poem as a drunk-text
        but to who? to god?   to some
invisible pantheistic reading committee?   it was
on CA-17 and in snatches when I wasn't thinking
about crashing   just as I'm trying not to
think about that right now   in the light of the
fact that this is basically over   closure and
disclosure   there on the 17 this poem was

something quite different but it is certainly the
same poem and that   is the most
intentional and explicit thing about it

5 Poems

Aidan Semmens

A Strange Geometry

after all these forty summers her face
now powder white
interrupts his nights

> her cold white face
>
> > bandied
>
> everywhere before him
> as he roams his little world
> swinging
>
> > between crutches

some storeys up, she descends into hell
– or is it escape? –
via the beckoning frame of a window

here then is the story
every story there is

the door hinged
to open either way

      she is no ghost
      for time is not present
      or past
            but is

yes, a window, geometric aperture
through which a woman – anyone –
may make an exit

      restlessly
          he moves
      among the arcane structures
      the complexity
           set out by men

but was it the window
he saw her face
reflected in
or staring blankly through?

the windows polished and shone
the windows broken
shattered in the streets
leaving mannequins and their owners
exposed, still, barefaced, blank

the trap does not spring shut
but closes slowly
         irrevocably
impermeable

      where one's head is arranged
      at another's foot
      he, wandering, must
      seem a malignant growth
            yet

with his callipers he goes
among and between
                              quartering

the planet

she leaves behind her
a kerfuffle of papers
as she takes her last exit
through the high casement

            swerving in continuum
                              void
            beyond and above
                        such a sphere
            is merely veering
                        amid nothing
            continuously: or time
            is only distance
                  movement

light from the window behind him
caught in his glasses
makes bright points on the paper

            stoppage or continuation
            departing or arrival
            he
                  lusts
            for climactic death; night
            strangely holds him
            but always
                        the earth turns anew
            to the sunrise
                        and his numinous
            visions are sent back
                              diseased
to wherever they came from

she contemplates again the imperfection
in the glass
        that bubble
where clouds wiggle

        should he select
                a door
      or wait for one
             to swing
      open in his direction?

seen from the bed, the window
is the scene of all life
all activity
      of birds and neighbours
tradesfolk and the curious unknown

      the strangest door
             is the one
that closes silently behind him
leaving him
         surprised
to find that all seems still
the same about him

the same

    and not the same

Dancers and Architects

on warm windless nights
the old termite mounds sparkle
with eerie green light
flashed by click-beetle larvae
living in the outer layers

you may be struck by the contrast
between the leaf's cool blue
and the light of the fire
seeping through the wound

shifting winds make flames of the dancing sand
lightning lacerates the sky, lava lighting
the swelling smoke
a breeze pushes the animals along
like tiny boats

elegant swimmers, they will glide
right into you, gently nudging
you out of their way, she says

waterlilies stretch up to the light
through a thick green layer of mist
in a once sacred sinkhole

low cloud covers the meadow
and apollos shelter among the grasses

the male pauses
in his pre-dawn display
tail and wings fanned and fluffed
against the backdrop of the forest

then turns his back on her
brushes her face with his wire plumes

the massive gorgonian coral shelters
by day a shoal of tiny cardinalfish

a geological event, extreme heat deep
within the continental crust
gave rise to the crystal formation

an almond tree where fireflies gather
patterns of light moving constantly
on the surface of a forest pool

planktonic animals nightdiving in deep water
contrasts in movement and texture
patterned fish sheltering among swaying tentacles

tangled silvery threads, the rivers
and deltas change from day to day
a firework display in slow motion
a giant puffball frantic with activity

tendrils coiled like clefs
on a musical stave

Goodbye Don't Mean I'm Gone

nothing that happens in the roadside cabin
is his doing or his choice

outside among the waiting men
the air is grey with condensed breath
and cheap smoke, fumes
from heavy engines slowly turning over
to retain a little warmth
and the illusion of readiness

few words are passed among them,
for some perhaps it matters
where the dead are buried,
on what patch of earth
the border line is drawn

Light Falls

not yet halfway to the summit
we pause to take in the view –
on a stretch of road near the power plant
abandoned vehicles swallowed
by trees and grass, a chained-up motorbike
absorbed into the land

above perhaps raptors or ravens
and a stray gleam
of something you can't make out
or tiny icicles of breath
caught in the shining air

dust of the country, dust of the town
weave together on the wind

where a traveller might stumble
on an ancient site
old men sit under arches, tombs
robbed of artefact and bone

places have voices not their own
yet I am snatched back
to a land of lawns, sunset malls
coldest recorded winters
the room dark and a man
writing, moving his hands

the lost game of self
and making it all up

we watched the news
with the sound turned down
on secular transcendence

of falling towers, tear-streaked
infants in bombed-out plazas
migrants at the gates
of a gated hell
crusts in their multilingual hands
at the alarm-wired portal
the revelations of February
triumphs of industry and agriculture
a glimpse behind the scenes at the congress
splendid acts of desecration

you say nothing we remember today
may be of significance tomorrow
to see is not to understand
things photographed or passed over
old texts that speak of mysteries
the sick asleep in temple sanctuaries
for fear of the image
reification of the word

a pale sky scratched by contrails
erasures in the view
misleading shadows
uninterpretable space
impressions of movement and gradations
of light travelling obliquely
casting reflections glistening
on sea or city streets

and how we learn what happened here
in passing fragments, not quite believing
or not wanting to believe

Thirty-four Statements Amounting to a Definition

Unseen dangers lurk beneath the grassblades of your lawn.

A mountain cannot be trusted to remain where it is mapped.

The blackbird does not know how closely its song resembles Mozart's 40th symphony.

At one moment the number of mobile phones equalled the number of living alligators.

The patterns of motorway traffic may be described as a form of Brownian motion.

The motion of bees may be discerned in shopping malls.

A man has reached adulthood without ever having a name.

There is a woman who has never been seen.

The piano was invented in Bolivia in the year 1216.

There are several species of worm that breed only in the catacombs of Paris.

This former jihadi and publican is now an itinerant bookseller.

This cola contains several unknown substances.

Some rainbows contain more colours than others.

A mistranslated copy of the Book of Genesis has been found in a cache of dinosaur bones.

Spinoza and Pocahontas became secret lovers in Brussels.

A mile below the Antarctic ice is a stone in the shape of St Basil's cathedral.

This ancient petroglyph may be decoded as a periodic table of elements.

From a certain angle, all inhabitable planets form a perfect image of the Mona Lisa.

For certain species all perceptible existence lies within the wavelengths we see as green.

In the basement of my house is an incalculable number of unexplored corridors.

The warm night conceals artworks and aardvaarks.

The bear you see in this picture is a 23-storey building.

These shoes were once worn by a Californian war-lord.

Most of the Earth's surface has been seen only by fish.

Communication has been achieved between Bratislava and Bangkok using an old nail file and a television set.

Piltdown Man was fluent in several Polynesian languages.

In certain Sumerian dialects the number three is unpronounceable.

The most intelligent person in the world is the fifth daughter of a subsistence farmer.

The colour vermilion is unknown in Letchworth Garden City.

Deep in the Mariana Trench lies a phonographic cylinder of Enrico Caruso singing Dixie.

St Anthony of Padua passed messages to the KGB hidden chemically in a phial of urine.

The relative acidity of Beethoven's concertos has never been accurately measured.

Plato and Aristotle scratched their names on the Berlin Wall.

It is impossible to prove whether the Mona Lisa winks when unobserved.

In some worlds this poem includes a thirty-fifth proposition.

from Dante's Purgatorio Canto XX

Philip Terry

I'd have happily gone on talking for a while longer,
But he'd had enough of my questions, so I
Left him where he lay, and put away my notebook,

The page unfilled. Berrigan negotiated
The track ahead, sticking close to the cliff,
Wherever there was space to tread,

For on the other side those sprawling shades,
Who distil in tears the greed that gobbles up
The planet, were too close to the drop for comfort.

"Fuck you capitalism, you couldn't give a shit
About anything except your profit margins!
Take a good look at your kind, crawling like worms

On the edge of this mountain, and tell
Me if any six figure bonus can help them now?
Your never-sated appetite has claimed more victims

Than any plague or famine or natural disaster.
When will the day come when we ditch you for
Good, like toxic waste in a bottomless landfill?"

We went on with slow and cautious steps,
My mind fixed on those shades that I heard
Grieving and sobbing so piteously.

Then I happened to catch a voice from
Somewhere up ahead wailing "Holy Mary!"
Like a woman off *Call The Midwife* crying out in labour.

And then right after: "How poor you were is
Plain from the lousy accommodation you
Shared when you dropped your sacred load."

And then I heard: "Ah, good Bullimore, you
Preferred to stay true to yourself on a miserable wage,
Rather than ingratiate yourself with the rich."

I was so intrigued by what I heard that
I quickened my pace to find the spot I
Thought the words were coming from, eager to

See the shade who had just spoken;
He went on, speaking of that generous
Philanthropist, Sylvia La Terre, who

Spent her fortune helping former sex workers
Find safe houses and independence.
"Hello," I said, "I couldn't help hearing your voice,

Tell me who you were, and tell me why you
Alone lie here praising generous hearts.
If you can give me an answer, then do,

And if I live to tell my tale back on earth,
Before my days are done I promise to put
In a good word for you among the living."

"I will answer you," he said solemnly,
"Not out of hope for any help from your world, but
Because of the balls you show in coming here at all.

I was the root of that malignant tree
Which overshadowed the oil industry
In the 1970s, from which no good fruit is plucked.

Even the princes of Saudi Arabia
Had nothing on me – so great was my wealth
I had them eating out of my hand.

I was known as Jean Paul Getty in the world: from
Me sprang those John Pauls the second and the third
By whom our business has recently been rocked.

I was the son of an attorney in
The insurance industry, a shrewd man,
From whom I learned thrift and the value of oil.

At twenty-one I was given $10,000 to invest
In oil fields in Oklahoma. We struck oil within
A year and by the next August I was a millionaire.

I found the dynasty's reins clutched in my hands,
And its whole government, and so much power
That once I tasted it I cried out for more.

I had wished to place the business in the hands of
My son George, but he was a disappointment to me.
The pressure must have been too much for him,

So he turned to drugs, then took his own life
In the most horrible manner, stabbing
Himself to death with a barbecue fork.

Worse was to come. My grandson made a fool
Of us all with a photoset in *Playgirl*,
And ran up a huge debt in Italy over cocaine.

Worse was to come. In a botched attempt to
Pay off his debts he staged a kidnapping.
We knew right off there was something funny

About it all, and ignored the ransom requests.
I still don't know how it all came about,
But at one point what had all started off as

A bad joke turned bitter. In the sort of twist
Of fate that could only happen in Italy,
A group of upstart Calabrian Mafiosi

Kidnapped him for real. The ransom was absurd,
$17,000,000, and I refused to pay –
I didn't want to put the whole family in jeopardy.

Eventually we negotiated them down,
At no inconsiderable risk to myself, I could add.
I organised a loan, on generous terms,

For the boy's father, but he refused to sign.
He was another disappointment, another one
Who wasted his life dabbling in drugs.

Worse was to come. The boy's ear turned up in the post.
It was the last straw, so I decided to pay
Myself, going halves with the boy's father.

And that was that. He was returned to his
Family, minus the ear. I cut off all ties with the boy
After that and never spoke to him again.

Oh, avarice, what worse lies in wait for our family,
Now that we have become so close to you
We don't even care for our own flesh and blood?

To make the past and future look less dire,
I built the Getty Villa and the
Getty Centre, outside Los Angeles, by the sea,

To make a permanent home for my art collection,
And to carry out research into art history.
Though the vinegar and gall didn't stop here –

Critics called my Getty Villa vulgar
And compared it to Disneyland,
Then after this my wives drifted off,

One by one. I guess they could see my true
Love was oil – you either make a successful business
Or a successful marriage, you can't have both.

When you saw me back there, calling out to
Mary, that one true bride – that's what we
All do here while the daylight still lasts,

But when night falls we turn to greed for our theme.
In darkness, we call up Pygmalion, who murdered his
Sister Dido's husband, to fill his pockets with gold.

We tell how Midas suffered when his miser's prayer
Was answered, how he starved as his food turned
To gold, how he ended in ludicrous despair.

Then we remember Achan, who stole the spoils
Of Jericho, and was stoned to death for his sacrilege.
There's a striking painting of the scene in the Jewish

Museum in New York, by Joseph Tissot,
You should check it out if you ever go there,
And there's Blake's version too, 'The Blasphemer'.

Then we accuse Sapphira and her husband,
We praise the hooves that kicked Heliodorus,
Then the Essex Alp resounds to the infamous

Polymnestor, who murdered the boy Polydorus,
As Virgil tells. Last of all we cry: 'Crassus,
Tell us, for you know, what flavour does gold have?'

At times one of us calls out loud, while another
Whispers softly, as the urge takes us. We are
Like Quakers here, and only speak when moved

To do so. So when I called out in praise
Of those generous spirits, I was not alone as
You thought, it was just that others held their peace."

We had already left that shade behind,
And leaning on our sticks struggled as best we could
To make progress across that difficult terrain,

When suddenly, as though jelly moulds were
Crashing down from the high walls of Hell's
Kitchen, I felt the mountain quake and tremble,

At which point an icy coldness clutched me,
As it clutches one that goes to his death.
The Millenium Bridge never shook so violently

Before the engineers at Arup shored it up
With inertial and fluid-viscous dampers.
Then all around we heard calamitous shouts,

So loud that Berrigan, my guide, drew close
To me, and held me tightly in his arms: "Just keep
Cool," he said, "I'm not going to let you down now."

"Let's party!" they all shouted together,
And "Dude!" as I could hear from those nearest,
Whose shouts were clear enough to make out.

We stopped and waited for the commotion to pass,
All the while the ground trembling beneath our feet,
Until the quake ceased and the cries died down.

Then we continued on our solitary road
Still gazing at the shades prostrated on the ground,
Who once more began their Quaker's round.

13 Ways of Looking at the Lives of the Artists

Kat Peddie

[*A series of alternative interpretive texts for Winifred Nicholson's* The Artist's Children, Kate and Jake, at the Isle of Wight *in the Bristol City Museum and Art Gallery.*]

1

Winifred and Ben Nicholson have been flattening the plane. Later he will leave the figurative, though not entirely. It is an old value. Ben Nicholson is becoming a major artist. He has put away childish things. He has come of age and the family is flattened. Look at the children's faces.

2

The husband has moved into abstraction this
is what they are left figuring out

3

When I fell in love with Barbara Hepworth it was like falling in love with pure form and the knowledge that form is never pure. The sculptural dome of her forehead and its environments! The hollow children are probably innocents. They cannot compete with this. It is not fair to make them.

4

Further down the line, I will make a version of the story where Barbara Hepworth will leave Ben Nicholson for her studio.

5

A friend of mine, who is an artist and a mother and has lived longer than me, says that it would not then have been possible to leave the father of your triplets. It does not happen this way round.

6

When I started, I was not thinking about children, and now there are so many of them. The way they keep looking at me, and with those eyes.

7

You are an observer of your family. You are not the only one. I also look in and the children stare back. Someone has to compose the family, don't they?

8

In a parallel line, Barbara Hepworth leaves John Skeaping for Ben Nicholson. She takes their child and he paints pictures of horses. I don't mean to say we don't all suffer. We do.

He never thinks about what name to put to the painting and it is the only one that I can never quite remember.

9

This is a mother and child painting. This is the image of western art. Now that the mother paints she can move outside the frame.

10

The frame is so heavy. Is this what you wanted? The family is so hemmed in.

11

Hold the family tight. Don't let in too much landscape. Outside there is too much of it to look at.

12

This is a still life with children and landscape.

The children are the middle ground. It would be difficult to paint this another way.

In the foreground, the still life rounds out.

Still, life moves. A child is having a birthday. A cake does not belong in a still life so the children must eat fruit. Still, observe the girl's jaunty hat!

13

The hat is too large to be jaunty, or the girl too small.

Tone is achieved by an accumulation of angles, scale, children. Observe the broad brush strokes, the way the coast behind them is actually the Isle of Wight!

14

The girl barely has eyes. She will become an artist.

15

The children are unhappy. You cannot stop them from feeling this. Already they have gone beyond you, though the girl has yet to fully take on form.

16

and maybe you hold them or yourself to yourself or the light and ask: does this child spark joy?

and the painting?

17

'By this I mean the power to create individual shapes that have, even apart from their relations with each other or with other shapes, a taut vitality of their own.'

- David Baxandall, *Ben Nicholson*

18

The boy is more fully realized.

19

and if you ask your children to express yourself it is probable they will fail and call it survival and that this might be something like the lives of the artists, which, please observe the broad brush strokes, could also be called the lives of others.

Disturbed

Toby Olson

1

The genesis of all that rocks the waves
so that the character of flotsam in their curls
when found at surf side
is examined in curiosity and not wonder
       becoming the way of it
those lost chances for the vision
that precedes understanding
so that light coughing in public galleries
where quiet background music is Chopin
while a fog in the civilized head
calls for quiet appreciations
as turbulent oceans on canvases
in elaborate frames
hide their genesis.

2

He remembers the house on the hill
where quiet background music is Chopin
and he is once again in shorts and halter
while mother touches his brow
over and over again
so that he shivers in pleasure and the annoyance
that precedes understanding
as food turns foul in the mouth
where a boy stands in pajamas
ready for bed and aloneness
but for his chicken and rabbit
while the bell in the toy church
rings out death
over and over again.

3

The sea-side marshes are flooded
over and over again
as the oceans deposit their ships' wealth
among weeds and flowers
where fish now struggle in fresh water
and sunset rings out death in the voices
of remaining gulls
who head for their meals or nesting
        while among the living
the dead rise up accusingly in memory
in night's shadows in lamp light
and guilt foolishly comes to roost
as food turns foul in the mouth
of those who feed upon death.

4

But now the mother is dead
and he is forty-three
in night's shadows in lamp light
whereupon a table holds his whiskey
that he might be oiled for reading
these books of those who feed upon death
in a history before his own
while among the living
politics rages
and there is no power in those
caught up in the maelstrom
as the dead rock in somebody's paradise
while hell is only a vague promise in books
as he raises his glass.

5

Caught up in the maelstrom
and white clouds hung low
over the bay's unshadowed majesty
the bait fish rose turbulent to the surface
in futile escape from the death below
while gulls squawked in the air
announcing death's presence
a feast for the fishermen who
        in this sad half natural cycle
gathered on waves in aggressive circles
again and again in view
of that house on the hill now vacant
as the sea held sway as witness
in a history before his own.

6

In futile escape from the death below
there are turbulent explorations
        and wet hair under his arms
in Chet Baker's honey in the livingroom
where there are surf-stones
numbered and dated
in artistic piles that are sea tossed
and a messy abstract hung on the wall
in this sad half natural cycle
their juicy pleasures
and he knows she has him
        locked away from his taste
as clay animals strut on the mantle
and a shorn Poodle licks away at his toes.

7

Numbered and dated
the ships march out across the Atlantic
invisible beyond sight from the yearning shore
where there are surf-stones
and the mysteries inside the ships
are sea tossed
and mystery is memory
as much as the shuffling cargo
is scuttling towards its own future
while this drama's story
might reach out and touch the ships
even as the sea-side watchers
picnic or lie in the sun
and take delight in the empty waves.

8

This is about a man who returns
to the beach of his childhood at sixty-seven
where there are numbered stones
          scattered in the sand
and the vacant house on the hill
is the dead past
and about a confusion of papers
on a desk where he spends his life
in the construction of other lives
          so that all else becomes illusion
and he might think of the grave yard
as he imagines his mother
in the house on the hill above
gazing at the sea through windows.

9

And behind his mother's face
is the face of the wife that has joined her
so that all else becomes illusion
as he whittles away at the days
a glass of bourbon
among the scatter of papers on the desk
where time meanders
in the construction of other lives
while the body confronts its slow collapse
and he can hardly rise to reach his pencil
though he is strong enough
to confront his reading
and the confusion of dead characters
in the book beside the bourbon.

10

And in the book a man travels
into various tortured circumstances
        sets off to sail upon a distant sea
and discovers the rotting cargo
where time meanders
while paragraphs are both repeated
and created in his mind
at the edge of sleep
so that all else becomes illusion
and the cargo in his head
becomes the story
of loss and pathological longing
that lingers in the sleeper's imagination
as the book ridicules the reader.

11

And yet he is forced to the stories
that he has created
and the ones still to be brought
to a kind of life that is not life
though in time there will be an ending
and the cargo in the head will rot
as the story teller becomes the story
of loss and pathological longing
but for the bourbon
that sits among papers
and brings an appropriate dullness
to the one who is dealing in machination
as the desk is facing the window
through which the sea is unconcerned.

12

Once again the sea confronts the story
with disregard
as the sailor unfurls his canvas
upon which no words are written
and the bluefish school
at the ankles of the oyster picker
and the surf licks the toes
of the beautiful maidens
while far out and beyond vision
whales breach and blow
in those hours of the day
when the sea is placid
and holds their massive bodies
gently caressing them.

13

And so does he come to be eighty
and becomes the story
of a teller of limited ability
who nevertheless tells his stories
here on the Cape in May and sunlight
          where silence is a reminder
that the time is short
and all the while I am leaving
my bed at 4 am
drinking coffee and remembering
that I love that past
in which I meet my people once again
admire their power in the memory
and write about them.

14

The sea is calm tonight
as seen from his window
and there are soft lights in fog
in the town out at the hook
      and people might be dancing there
or sitting at restaurant table
overlooking the placid waters
while house lights blink
along the curve of shore
and motors on the highway are trivial
as the fenders are still
at the gunwales of boats at the dock
yet the distance between us as always
is the wild uninterested sea.

from *LIGHTSAIL*

Lissa Wolsak

SOME APPREHENSION KEEPS US

OVERAMPING..

LOUD

IN SO SAYING,

GAINS AND LOSES BREATH

HOW THIS ALSO ENDED AN

ELECTROMAGNETIC DELIRIUM ..

TO VIVIFY WHERE

THEY HAD THEN SHIMMIED

TO BECOME COLD

FIRE

SO IT WAS .. TO

STRIP THE BELLS OF THEIR

SOUND

WE ..

AWAITING THE

NUMINOUS CONVERSATION THAT

NEVER AROSE..

AND FOR THAT

WHICH MADE THE

BODY WEAKEN ITS

OPIATED TENOR,

ITS PUBLIC CRIB-MIND ..

ITS ENTIRETY, TO

BE WANTING..

WALK ON BY,

NOLI ME TANGERE

FOR, ROLLING

THE EGGHEAD

FROM HAVENS

HERE AND THERE

WIELDS IDOLATRY

AND BY SUCH

ESSENCELESSNESS,

LIKE INSECTS .. USES

A STORM TO BREED,

IN ITS MIDST

MAKING AGAIN

THE SINEWY USURIES

THESE TOILS MISSING THE

CURVATURE

UNDERSENSED

AHEAD

BLOODTHRONG

DRAWING BLEARY CIRCLES THERE ..

THEY BURN WITH A MOODY, INVERTED REVERENCE

BUT WHEN GIVEN SLEEP I THOUGHT THEM

FOUNDERING, FOG DRIP

ON QUIET STEEPS

FAR ON IN THE GLOAMING

TELLURIC ANATHEMA,

CUTTING THE VERMILLION

WAVES I HEARD

A SOFT WHISTLING, A

RUSTLING SOUND

INDUCING MURMURS ..

OUR ENTRANCE A

PRIVATE PARLAY, TA'WIL..., WE

FIRST FELT KINAESTHESIS TOWARD

UNDERSTANDING..

NEVER TO RETURN

TO MERE

AGREEMENT

CO-MOVING AS IT WAS,

SO WAS IT HERE

OUR EYES STOOD LOOSE..

THE DELICATE STRANGER

HUES TREMBLING

UNOPPOSED

INTO ITS SUBSTANCE

AND TURNING TO IT

OUR SUBJECTS LED US NATURALLY

WITH FEELING AND INTIMATIONS

AS EPHEMERAL ROPES OF SAND,

RELENTLESSLY

LIGHT-LIKE

UNAFRAID OF

MOTION

SHRILL AND TOO

BRIGHT THE TIPSTAFF..,

TETRAHEDRONALLY SACRED

OUR MUTILATED NATURES

DO CARE, LATE,

LATE VISIONS KNIT

AHEAD OF EACH OTHER'S

PUSH HAND,

TRANSLUCENT PATHWAYS

GROWN REEDY

WITH MINUTES TO IMPART

THE SUSURRANTS ..

SUPER-LUMINAL IN

MAKING EYE CONTACT

IN A PRIVATE HOUSE OR BY FUNNELING

INFLECTING TO THE

EARED

SUPPOSE

THE LEPER WENT ON

OR BROKE THROUGH..

USING ZERO-ENERGY ONTOLOGY

EASING THE SYMBIOSIS,

MAKING AND

RULING OUT

HER OWN NAME

WANTING PHYSIOCRACY

TO PLUMMET ITS OMNIPOTENT

CLOYING PUTTIES,

GO ALMOST

UNSEEN &

FORSAKEN

FOR BEING TO INTENSIFY

SHE WITHDREW INTO

INTIMACY

FATHOMING PRIMES..

TO IRIDESCE AGAINST THE

VAGARIES OF TRANSMIGRATION

SHE GREW ROSES

TO PROVIDE

OPTICAL CAVITIES

AFFORDING AMBIGUITY

WHICH ANIMATES

CO-MERCY

HOMO CAPEX DEI

CAPABLE OF THE

COSMOS,

PEOPLE KNOWING

EVERYTHING AT ONCE

S1: Holt

Sarah Hayden

What butters the cracks between what I hear myself speaking
and how it is I am heard? Show me how it grows. The l'ttle pause
between place and The Pale. Of what germ/ to what end. That I
might be so unrecognisable to my/self. What, tell me, is it made of?
Show me how it is pulled. Over and back, back, and over. <They say
they are changing the tapes> When the after/word cannot be borne,
I hum to me, swaying. With/through/by these moves,   find myself
carried across th'im/passes.

**<I think that the words forming in my mind are somewhat
detached from my normal thinking process>**

Wonder, then
And, as though she's singing: swaying.

Chanteuse. Rabbitlike.
A/n ear tipped toward th'earth, as though it could scoop up what
matters. Meaning. Let me just tune me in.
She sang so well it was like/ she was a___.

<'We are witness', the good doctor observes 'to an extraordinary image of distraction'i>

Audio/visual
In not hearing, looking extra hard
In not having what to hear, seeing it tremblesome.

Is it that she is trying to find the rhythm in her words but they have her instead, & in her body, just like that?
That, in speaking, she is already listening?
In speaking: timetravelling?

*

A__
        speech, sometimes, a/b times—
Feelings
rising
from off assembled heads.
Smiling at her own, at the joke against, with her
Is it maybe the lowered eyes and the smile that make it look like we should be hearing a song?

<On testing, it proved *very* lossy>

*

Prepositions [we say] are hard. Those inescapable relations. No position outside of in/ to. At this proximity, no absolutes. And yet, here we are, a longside, B-side, with and both in. Having been, both, out. A Door, /I/ A Door.

Nouns, now [at least here], stay roughly where they are, though taking on, as they might, diverses aspectes. But the prepositions? *Hyper*contextual & unstilling. This with, then. The work a so-calling Gemeinschaftsarbeit.
What with even *is* this?
        The file, I resave, renaming it Holtfilm, for I can hear/see no Serra here

*

In TNaG, France, the wonder, child switches tongues like radio channels.

In/frequencies, infrathins. In real cross-axial spinthrough.

The wonder, child, is making my head spin. These twill ears, with delay.

He finds no singlechannel synonym.

<It is a constantly revolving involuting experience>

Shade of my voicing. Revenant. Reviled. Shame of it. In speaking, I hear you as though across some blockage__breaking. I am un/sure that something. Un   sure what it is I have said. But there is none of you in this difficulty. It is only **<my own words pouring back in on top of me>**. For shame, for shame. Inconversation inechoic.

<What horrifies, is that we are present in this extended instant of her being so vulnerable with her/self>

*

//tensechange
TMP
cheek of the transposition//

*

The boys came early to the bureau today. In stillmisty hope that Dédé Sunbeam might be somewhere about. At the rue de Grenelle redux, they arranged themselves round the navel's mahoginnic inheritance and co-fantasised it for a camping table. Folded themselves quite in around it and prepared together (though in proper hierarchic formation) the Plan of Day.

Having pulled her from the library, they would propel her smartly into the transcription chamber. What they would do, in so far as would prove possible (and their predictions, all, diverged on this point) is have her wear the Special Headset. Then they would initiate

the procedure and record her reactions. Péret was elected to play stenographer. It was going to be
just fascinating.

Dédé, on capture, proved tricksier than they remembered—slash— than had been allowed for in the schedule. As it turned out, what with all her questions [*and all*], there was time for just 10 minutes of recording. There followed, by consequence, grumbling   but it wasn't to be helped.

Notwithstanding this, that, the results themselves *were* edifying. Even when, amid the planned meddling, it seemed like she might stop altogether, remove the device and go back to her reading— their cajoling, her general decency kept the thing on spoool.

*

Observe:
Listening, just, the girl and then the woman
Nodding like, as though someone asked for sage, parsley
<My I key ceases to function with any consistency. I am re, de-ceived>

Observe:
She's turning
& it's cut
She's turning....

Lift of the face, neatest nod and she's in class, soliciting what the raised hand prefaced.

Observe:
Chin up, and she's turning, chin up and she's turning back
The question, with a tint of petulance, the eyes thereafter, hurting

<If I look at you like this, you will know what it is you have done>

Insolent end of the face, turned Brucie, turned Mouthlike
Pointing, then, dirt under the nails

Chin, turn, this dance, this__

Resolve, readiness, this   rebeginning
Same sounds, coming round
Pause, fricative
Rebegins.
Light warrior. Rabbit mystic.
Dédé speaks from out (out of this world) from where the creatures
do be, being. Behind, that blue, the whole with gold leavèd.

*

"Miss Sunbeam's eyes", notes one naturalist, "flicker leftright like/as
though at th'wateringhole".
"Exacte!" shouts his oldest friend, cutting now cross-species; "she is
a very snake!".
Well, but of course. Or if not here, where?

To expedite publication, content-production was limited. Syllables
too, for the pain of them.

*

Back at the RdG:
One reporter gives over most of his allotment to the play of
illumination. A   celestial field retroactively intact. Somewhere
behind: a memory of his mother advancing (toward [no to] him, &
who else?) The light would take her like that, too. Hair-Halo-ed, it
being so given to transports of great sentiment. Its floating. Beyond:
Softness of the underchin, s/lightly. The generous yield.

<Shine a buttercup & you could eat her for breakfast. Sunbeam:
spread>

An/other, thinking himself well-trained in heavy symbols, fixes—
slash—fixates on the teeth. Jeunefille. Sexy, see?

Observe:
Our guide

as thoughasthough conscripted into spinning this brave mission.
Like: beyond the jungle's edge, but not in a helmet, no, not like that.
And yet, the transistor pickups are making her more rabbit/like than
anyone anticipated.
Flash partflash//

**<I think that the words forming in my mind are somewhat
detached from my normal thinking process>**

*

Say:
Snowblind
Whiteout topdown
The crown quite as it came
With the swirl that would make for kinks
The centre of her face: a girl's
That, or innocence

<Omg oso 70s>

We are finding our/
selves sillier than *anyone* had anticipated

       & all that blue__

Tongue as a slow weight. Clod.
Tongue now as salve,
uh   pology, the lips,
uncomprehendingly, ashamed.
Long lahs! Heavy fall.

*

After 2 years, Dr Krauss notes that she 'has great difficulty
coinciding with herself as a subject'.[ii] And three years there/or/after,
the EVP himself admits that 'In a very detailed and clear way, she
states what is happening to her as it is happening: her relation to
herself as subject'.[iii]

AUDIO TROUBLE

the letters rubber and jaunty as to the line.
This is not biting the lip. This is   resting the teeth a while,
immordantly.

As to: the piece piece__
For clues:
The body: Heavylidded, hers alone. She 'made herself its willing and
eloquent subject'.[iv]

Voice, too, even as she feels it come loose from her [sense of
her] self. Its wonder, its ill-suppressed incredulity, its slowing in the
attempt to cleave to the track, even as it lays it out.
<My I key ceases to function with any consistency.   I am re,
de-ceived>

SPON_TAN

These thoughts through which we are made with: all *them*.
Her resolve. Her pouring or being poured. Her pourformance.
<elbow-to-elbow. mine/yours//mirr/ors>

*

And the boys? Messing about in the backroom. Subsequent to some
giddy conspiring. **'So now since they're changing tapes'**, times
slip back out of forced alignment. The nows, thens. A   jumble.
Here, and here again, right now while just
after.
Can thinking slow? Does it, not rather, thicken?
The end's now.
Presents collapse.

Not knowing if I have heard me right, I move to swing out of the
light—hoping for transliterated silence.
Pickup.

In wonder to be sounding so different inside and out
or

In surprise at not being by oneself understood

Again: tipped to/ward th'earth. Another Plumbline.

I want // to hear
Amarillo, do you receive? Will you find it iterable?

---

[i] Rosalind Krauss, 'Video and Aesthetics of Narcissism', *October* (Spring 1966): 53.

[ii] Krauss, 53.

[iii] Richard Serra in Annette Michelson, Richard Serra, and Clara Weyergraf, 'The Films of Richard Serra: An Interview' *October* 10 (Autumn 1979): 83.

[iv] Krauss, 52.

All emboldened text spoken by Nancy Holt in Nancy Holt [& Richard Serra], *Boomerang* (1974).

3 Poems

Daphne Marlatt

first take

'The Crag" is an hotel (owned by the Runnymede) up on the Hill. It is over 2000 ft. up & is reached by a railway (really it is a glorified lift operated on the same lines as those at Hastings).... As you go up the railway, a wonderful scene unfolds itself & when you get to the top the air is delightfully cool & refreshing....

November 15th 1933

your tourist take on
the Hill as "here" then later
where home was

the storied Crag
is nowhere now

your letter back to Sutton
summons a misty

child memory tiffin
amid verandah drinks
(in) the view

there post-war?

early bungalow
built by East India captain
enlarged by the Sarkies'
grand Armenian hotel vision

first their E. & O.
below on Farquar St.
not to mention their Raffles
in Singapore

the Crag simply a "cool
retreat," ghost-story drenched
greenery above, around
bats' squeak

now in Brown's 1933
black-&-white online
I envision you walking
that sandy road to the Crag's
enormous staircase
filmed as a French *Indochine*
rubber plantation
later the ex-pat club of
Simla *Indian Summers*

now Empire's ruin
"don't go down that path"
where wild dogs & troupes
of raucous monkeys forage
through jungle's abundant
sun-filtered plenty

nostalgia for what no longer exists can't be
home-longing estranged sauntering the Summit
among Asian family weekend visitors come
up for the cool where small stalls offer trinkets
history's a faded sign-board noodle food court
reigns supreme

where off Tunnel Road
3 small girls hung back in the
orang gaji walkway to watch
that fierce jungle cat prowl
up to the family dog bowl
on the terrace of what we thought
was home

---

spatial immediacy and temporal anteriority
not only the photograph

*an illogical conjunction of the here-now and
the there-then*

felt

nostalgia's shadow image visceral imprint

just after the sun had set

*I felt almost like crying ... for there was a queer light everywhere &
the sea strangely reflected the light from the clouds... still caught by
the sunlight. Just then everything was suddenly so still & I could look
down into the darkening valley beneath me where the trees were
standing up absolutely without movement. Somehow it seemed as
though the whole of life were waiting in a tense suspense to receive
the last blessing of the departing day.*

November 15th 1933

shades of...

dark a dropped blind
though sea light reflects
the Strait

one long-held breath then

*one by one the twinkling lights of the Town...
so close they could have been almost at my feet*

young colonial giant
alone in that strange, that complex

as if touch

as if touched to the quick

Indira's net of light
you could almost see

your (no)self caught
up in

topical and tropic

The international position looks very unhappy at the moment.
Germany's declaration that she will build up an Army may have
serious consequences. It makes me speculate about undesirable
possibilities.... if we were in trouble in the West & Malaya were
left undefended, it would be a great temptation for Japan to step
in & take control here.... surely the Nations of Europe are not so
crazy as to allow themselves to become embroiled in another futile
recurrence of 1914!

March 20th, 1935 Penang

outlook
not the same as
look out

forward-looking not
the same as looking forward
(to)
　　　　spring not spring as in
　　　　England's less *gaudy*

... just breaking upon us here. The angsana trees are becoming
a blaze of yellow blossom, filling the air with perfume & covering
the roads with a mantle of gold. Outside my bedroom window are
masses of white temple flowers that make the night air heavy with
an exotic odour which will always remind me of Tamil temples. Then
we have the vermillion flame of the forest making a really dazzling
display, so profuse are its blossoms.... One is truly left with the
reflection that 'only man is vile'.

still March 20th, 1935

angsana eyes satiate this
sense drenched *here* you
record

despite incoming
history flowers destruct
destroy

browning edges of
frangipani wreaths their
continuance after death

(Mayan blooms in stone)

what does?

history re-cycles
never learn

now this here this coast's
bioregional fear
the pipe, the line's

imperial demand
work / oil

not rubber, tin
occasion war

"a culture is built from its
environment
                but a colonial
civilization lays its culture
over the environment"

          Roger Fernandes, S'klallam
          storyteller

3 Poems

Tania Hershman

Making Tea In Semi-Darkness

is ridiculous I spend the next several hours discovering that butter is
the absolute worst thing for my screaming fingertips instead dipping
them in and out of tepid water a glass by the bed while I'm not
sleeping I wonder why the hell I didn't just turn the light on what is
my problem with illumination why do I shrink from brightness

Fed

I say to the chef,
Make me something
with cheese. The chef

is my mother, my father,
my uncles and aunts,
the grandmothers

I never had. Wait
by the sea, says the chef,

so I sit in the waves
and I wave at the shells

and I shell up my heart
and I hearten my feet

with a fork in my hand,
and a spoon on my tongue.
Not long now, says the chef. Not long.

I am

part-leaf
        part-lake

and if you
        want me

to float
        and weave

skim air
        and take in

currents, I will be
        the lawns

your feet
        slide along

the bank
        you can never reach.

Toasters

Marilyn Stablein

Don't judge a toaster by its appearance.

A toaster's armor-like shell often gleams and sparkles but superficial reflections may hide a tumultuous inner life.

*

Before a toaster can fulfill expectations and perform the very basic mechanics of grilling, like most classes and species of beings, the male and female principles, the yang and the yin, must converge.

*

On a toaster the male element is represented by two or three metal-pronged projectiles found at the end of a long serpentine cord.

To activate the toaster the male prongs must penetrate the female receptacles mounted within a plastic or metal frame in a wall.

Only when male and female parts unite can the energy flow. To try to activate a toaster without a basic male-female conjunction would be futile.

*

When a slice of bread drops into one of the two open slots at the top of the toaster, a miniature elevator gently lowers the bread before the grilling unit. Rays of orangish light and auras of heat emanate from toasters confidently engaged in the act of toasting. A toaster's most important function is to generate this heat of transformation.

*

Exterior control knobs can adjust the timing and the degree of heat. Heavy, moist bread must languish longer before the radiating coils to achieve crunchiness.

Chance plays no role in toasting.

*

With a combination of symmetry, precision and balance, a toaster exposes bread to the glare of an inflamed electric wire coiled at just the right distance to singe only the surface.

The bread browns by degrees; a pale sesame deepens to a rich nutmeg.

*

Hot zig-zag coils emanate a brilliancy like molten lava. Heat permanently etches the bread.

Bread that touches or stands too close to a toaster's coils scars like a branded steer.

*

Some practices depend on repetitive motions, visions and/or sounds. For toasters repetition is equated with consistency.

Even the most base repetitive act is not without the possibility of engendering great passion.

*

With programmed mindfulness a toaster performs, time after time, in an enlightened way.

Repetitive acts offer opportunities to gain control or mastery.

*

The first round of toast takes longer to cook since the machine needs to warm up. Heat speeds up dehydration of the bread which accelerates the toasting. Subsequent slices lowered into preheated browning chambers cook faster and are more likely to overcook.

*

The ardor of toasters is self-evident in their willingness to radiate, to glow at the slightest provocation. Qualities of endurance and durability enhance a toaster's reputation.

Reluctance is not a quality of toasters.

*

Unpredictability is the Achilles' Heel of toasters, especially in relation to time and the mechanisms which govern the allotment of time.

The critical moment to disengage the heat—signaling the completion of the toasting process—varies not only from toaster to toaster but in the same toaster from one slice of pumpernickel to the next.

*

Never trust a toaster completely unless you are prepared to accept—it is unlikely but not impossible—the transformation of a decent slice of bread into a charred carcinogenic ruin.

*

At the first sign of smoke billowing from the toaster manually lift the elevator lever if there is one to eject the toast.

*

Disengage the male prongs from the female receptacles before inserting any tool or utensil into the chamber.

Jamming a knife or fork inside a toaster to pry loose a tightly wedged flaming slice of raisin bread is to risk death by electrocution and should be avoided.

*

Toasters, once activated, are self-regulating unlike motorcycles or vacuum cleaners. Toasters automatically disengage, or shut down, after completion of the operation for which they were constructed.

In this way toasters project stability and maintain independence.

Toasters do not abuse their autonomous status.

*

Depending on the degree of overgrilling—and the thickness of the bread—burnt toast may be salvaged by gently scraping off any sooty outer layer. If the toast charcoalizes—the end product of an errant and impassioned toaster—a knife scraped over the surface may dislodge some of the black crust.

*

In earlier times, during the heyday of toaster wizardry, a manufacturer's integrity guided specialists to assemble machines with only the finest parts.

Toasters lasted at the very least for the life of their owners, often longer.

Nowadays they malfunction after a year or two and often for no particular reason.

*

Neither abuse nor neglect but shoddy workmanship and cheap components are blamed for the systematic demise of a once flourishing line of well-crafted kitchen appliances.

New toasters are programmed for premature obsolescence.

*

Repairs are problematical. The older the toaster, the less likely a handyman can repair or replace broken parts. There are no guarantees nor warranties for outdated appliances. The bill to service a decrepit appliance can also be higher than the price of a new one.

*

There are few prospects for the preservation and maintenance of the aged. Death accompanied by the possibility of rebirth is one dimension—in an existence wrought with transcendent overtones—not available to toasters.

*

Once the intentionally short manufacturer's warranty expires, the only future for a defunct appliance is one found at the bottom of the trash heap.

No flowers or eulogies there.

Contempt and curses accompany the dead like squabbling buzzards.

Outside/Inside...Just Outside the Artworld's Inside, by Martha King
(Blazevox Books)

Ian Brinton

Memory is itself a form of story-telling and to some extent we all shape our pasts in the interests of our present. There are plenty of advanced literary critics today ready to talk of memoirs having 'a narrative truth' and language itself being doomed to unpunctuality with words chasing, describing and shadowing a reality that has already disappeared. In his fictional account of <u>A History of the World in 10 ½ Chapters</u> Julian Barnes had suggested that "History isn't what happened, it's what historians tell us happened". Or as his fictional school-teacher and narrator put to us in Flaubert's Parrot "How do we seize the past? Can we ever do so?" To give an example of the difficulty of ever reassembling the past or even grabbing firmly hold of what has in fact become history the narrator in that second novel recalls an anecdote from his college-days in which a piglet smeared with grease was let loose at an end of term dance:

> It squirmed between legs, evaded capture, squealed a lot. People fell over trying to grasp it, and were made to look ridiculous in the process. The past often seems to behave like that piglet.

Martha King knows the reality of this sliding world which is why she can say of her memoirs "Small surprise that what I remember is so indistinguishable from what I was told". In this fascinating compilation of moments covering some seventy years "Swarms of detail easily wrap themselves in clouds of false emotion" and memoir is always "a revision, a form of fiction".

In the early pages of the book Martha King suggests that memory as a movie "might use flashback techniques" and so when re-creating her wedding to the artist Basil King, Baz, she recalls that "premarital counselling" had been provided by John Wieners who had studied with Baz at Black Mountain College:

> The filmmaker should show us meeting on Columbus Avenue. John looked far younger than his age when he was young, and the man we encounter on the street is a delicate bird, with a prominent hook nose, smooth forehead, and curling dancing eyes. He will write all the work in *The Hotel Wentley Poems* three months from now. The book will be published a little later in the year. But we already know what a poet he is. And we're excited. We tell John we're getting married. But instead of smiling he looks worried. Then asks us each for our place and date of birth, which we give him. The time of day? We both guess. He pulls a pocket-sized astrology reference book from his inside jacket pocket. "You'll be fine," he says after ruffling some pages.

Among those flashbacks, those moments of reminiscence which stand arrested for a moment, for a lifetime, we meet Robert Creeley. He and Martha went on long walks from Black Mountain; they "walked and talked all night":

> I don't know if Bob told me then about his father's death, or if it was later that I got that defining image of the two dark tracks from the ambulance wheels that backed across his snow-covered front lawn and carried his dying father away. Tracks that stayed until the spring thaw. That backed across his heart. That stayed for a lifetime.

This was a conversational world in which the focus of discussion was upon process rather than arriving at conclusions and Black Mountain College promoted the growth of a language "that works at getting at things, making connections that might be generative, a risky language not focused on defending itself, ranking itself, not devoted excessively to maintaining prestige and position." The immense value that lurked behind that North Carolina educational venture, a campus that had hosted poets such as Charles Olson and Robert Duncan, artists such as Franz Kline and Willem de Kooning, musicians and experimental artists such as John Cage and Buckminster Fuller, can be felt in Martha King's account of the proposed New York exhibition promoted by the art critic G.R. Swenson. Two years after the death of Frank O'Hara in an accident on Fire Island Swenson had wanted to organize a "counter-salon show" which would reassert the centrality of art offering a blow against irony. Intensity, honour and commitment were to be exhibited as a challenge to the "Art-smarts" which could be so easily learned, the Pop art in which "new could be as easy as picking up an attractive comic book", the 1968 Art world which had toned down the dangerous qualities that had surrounded the earlier generation's art. Swenson arranged for his exhibition to be held in the main floor exhibition space at New York University's Loeb Student Center and it would promote work by Baz, Carol Haerer, Ivan Micho and Philip Wofford amongst others. A small manifesto was written for the exhibition under the title "Origins and Cycles" and the opening night was crowded with "friends and friends of friends". And then all went silent: there were no reviews and it was as if someone had hung a "don't touch it" sign up. The need to toe a party-line was further emphasised when Swenson's article for the catalogue of a big Museum of Modern Art exhibition of Jim Rosenquist's work was perceived by the establishment to be off-piste. Swenson poured out his rage and grief to Martha King and told her how he received a call from *Time* magazine offering him a guest column if he would "adjust" the views he had expressed in that catalogue. Swenson's admiration for Rosenquist's work was centred upon it constituting a blow against an artist's sense of ironic distance and Swenson made a strong case for irony being used "to mask a cynical dread of belief". Three years later Basil King was to publish parts of this essay in the magazine *Mulch* and its appearance there asserted the importance of what Martha was to call an art "that is exactly what you see", an art which is a "blow against hermetic, self-referential cleverness".

The presence of Baz haunts the pages of this remarkable memoir and the respect which Martha pays him is itself a testament to a life of shared artistic commitments. After a trip to England in 1985 Baz opened up his life as a writer and "soon he was writing a place for himself between writing and painting, bringing together disparate things which has always been his gift and his burden".

Martha and Basil King moved to Grand Haven in Michigan in 1972 when Baz took up a post at Thomas Jefferson College, a post which he owed to the encouragement of the dying poet Paul Blackburn. Martha wrote poetry:

> In Grand Haven I didn't have a money job. In the mornings, when the house emptied out, I went upstairs to the typewriter on a big wooden table at the end of the bedroom. Most of the poems in my New Rivers book were hammered out at that table while I sweated and swore and smoked cigarettes.

She wanted to use what she had learned from reading Olson about the resonance of a place being revelatory and "that out of a jumble of information – personal stories, devices, connections, extensions – could come *form*". Her poetry, so like this woven book of memoirs, reveals "the past's continual cryptic intrusion" and in 'Husband & Wife', an early poem from *Imperfect Fit,* the selected poems which was published in 2004 by Marsh Hawk Press, we can see the patterning taking place:

> to take command
> of the situation
> is the job of a weaver

In the opening essay to his book *Scratching the Beat Surface* Michael McClure had said that he wanted to "express the intensity and vividness of my own perceptions and the *manner* in which impressions linked themselves in the exciting swirl that I called my consciousness". Martha King's autobiographical memoir, both *Outside* and *Inside*, achieves precisely this and it recalls those words she had used in 'M to B', that celebratory poem to Baz in which she had acknowledged a lifetime of commitment:

>   This is a greeting from me
>   on your fifty-third birthday
>   not just a present sweep I'm using
>   to keep sorrow back
>   but a clear ring of words you might speak
>   as you step up onto the street

"through my hand to you": Hank Lazer's *Brush Mind: At Hand*

Sara Wilson

Dedicated to the great calligrapher and Zen teacher Kazuaki Tanahashi and written with a special brush pen given to the poet by Buddhist priest and poet Norman Fischer, Hank Lazer's *Brush Mind: At Hand*, as the title implies, is an examination of how a spiritual practice that reforms and recalibrates one's mind in the act of calligraphy is "at hand." That is, the "brush mind," a phrase referencing Tanahashi, is "here" in the existence of the physical book, but is also actively found "at hand," in the act of reading and writing calligraphy. In this significant variant from his handwritten shape-writing Notebook projects, Lazer opens up Tanahashi's teaching on the brush mind to those unfamiliar with it while adding his own distinctly American flavor, making Western Zen and Judeo-Christian philosophy accessible even in the time it takes to read the book—a mere 7 minutes (or longer), leading some to call it "flash poetry."

 Brush Mind: At Hand is a sampler of poetic snapshots, a fresh, humorous, casual yet profound collage of insights. My first encounter with Lazer's unassuming work was at a poetry reading. Lazer showed the audience some of the pages of his book, poking fun at what he called his "childish writing"—a reference to the book's handwritten, calligraphic style of writing rendered in thick black strokes that fill each 8.5"x 11" white page. Lazer charmed us with his familiar voice and slow-paced performance of his poetry, which ranges from the philosophical to the colloquial. Each turn of the page reveals what appears to be a completely new thought. We move from

it

didn't

hit me

until

much later

to the following page:

Maybell

had Cooter's outfit

picked out

before

he was cold

The colloquialisms join together what many may consider to be very different strands of knowledge: Western Zen and East Asian traditions, American common sense—"it's always one thing or another"—and Judeo-Christian spiritualities (while also pointing to yoga practices): "oh child you / are doing / the ministry / of the body / which yes / is one / of the temples." In its joining together of wisdoms and spiritualities, it claims a kind of grandeur, reducing cultural and spiritual particularities into a general meditation on ontology. While it condenses rigorous religious traditions down to its simplest (often, American colloquial) linguistic units, perhaps erasing particularity, *Brush Mind* also makes it possible for each spiritual tradition to speak to one another in a non-exclusive, non-binaristic way. The quality and tone of this poetry allows each page to breathe on its own while making clear its place in a constellation of American thought. Rather than joining "the" East and "the" West together, *Brush Mind: At Hand* reflects on a very American compilation of thought, influenced by and pointing back to philosophical ancestries in other cultures, certainly, but nevertheless involving a distinctly American transpacific stream of consciousness, as when the page "nothing / in / particular" points to content steeped in Zen philosophy

while its linguistic arrangement is Anglo-American with a significant
Alabama element to it.

Aside from the charm of the poetry itself, its handwritten
style makes this a personal experience: reading the book feels as
if you have stumbled upon someone's poetry/writing journal. This is
a book that makes manifest its own cautious thinking through the
care with which we see the calligraphy was traced and the quiet
ways in which the text asks the reader to turn each page. It is also
an examination of language, not just in its simple presentation of the
colloquial but also in slight commentary, as in:

> after
> i am
> gone
> word loop
> keeps running

A rather heavy philosophical fragment, this points to how subjects
are born into language and that the system of language, a "word
loop," will "keep running" even after death. But there are also
contemporary truisms—"this / moment / is / your / life"—that
punctuate the work, pointing us back to mainstream cultural values
and perhaps questioning the value of such clichés at the same time
that the work bravely grants them importance. "this / moment / is
/ your / life" is followed by "& then / you begin / again / to hear /
your thinking," adding a self-conscious, self-reflexive element to the
cliché.

Though the book as medium and the act of turning a page
suggest a kind of development or end, Lazer's work resists teleology
at the same time that the poetic fragments feel connected. One
could take each page as a poem unto itself, but the rest of the
pages make each specific page significant. Like language, each
page gains meaning by those surrounding it. And yet these pages
do not really belong together, either—syntactically, narratively, and
logically, they don't follow. *Brush Mind: At Hand* allows for multiple,
non-hierarchical entry and exit points. Each page has its own poem,
its own little world of text, recalling Lyn Hejinian's singular sentences
in *My Life*, ostensibly atomized pieces linked together in paragraphs
that mimic prose but at the same time resist the growth of a larger,
paragraph-sized meaning that a reader would expect to develop with

the reading of each new sentence. Much like Hejinian's larger work coalesces into an impressionistic sense of an autobiography, Lazer's poetry begs to be read to the end, and upon reaching the book's last page, there is a satisfaction unavailable if the book is read in bits and pieces. Each piece, or page, thus belongs the others.

There are multiple entry points as well in the many mediums of *Brush Mind*: though my first encounter was primarily aural, since then I have gotten my hands on a beautiful paperback copy and viewed Lazer's video collaboration with Jane Cassidy, Michael Harp, Aaron Dues, Andrew Raffo Dewar, and Holland Hopson. In this video version, the charming colloquialisms take on new hues, with multiple musical frames overlaying one's visual experience of each "page"—in this case, each still. The text of *Brush Mind: At Hand* loops through three times, with a different musical track for each version, and due to this looping, the "reading"/viewing experience of the video stretches out to around thirty minutes, as opposed to the sort of flash-poetry feel of the paperback book.

Kazuaki Tanahashi has asked, "if each stroke is our entire breath, how dare we correct it?" Lazer plays with this question while nodding to Charles Olson's projective verse, with its focus on "certain laws and possibilities of the breath, of the breathing of the man who writes as well as of his listenings," which in turn owes much to Ezra Pound's insistence that a poet compose her work "in the sequence of the musical phrase, not in sequence of a metronome." This insistence on stroke and breath is certainly apparent in the reading of the hard copy; each poetic phrase is punctuated by the turning of the page, where each page contains just a fragment of a sentence, allowing about one breath per page. But the sequencings of text and music in the video/installation plays even further with this attention to breath, music, and rhythm, removing from the viewer the ability to turn the page, instead surrounding each poetic fragment with music and perhaps pushing viewers to breathe and listen in new ways.

The first "version" of the video *Brush Mind: At Hand*, composed and played by Michael Harp and Aaron Dues, is framed by music that is electronic in its musings, dreamlike, expansive, perhaps pointing to the cosmos. It is the kind of music you wish would underscore your experience in an aquarium, watching in awe as the most vibrantly-colored underwater creatures glide by the glass. In the video, each fragment's color composition is that of white calligraphy against a black screen (rather than the opposite, black calligraphy against a white page, in the hard copy). A shift occurs with each new iteration of *Brush Mind*, just as a shift also occurs when the text directs itself toward "you," as in "I think / I told / you / think / light / years" or "you don't / decide / what you / are / thinking," among other phrases. The few "you"-directed panels created a kind of a personal interrogation, playing with the idea that calligraphy has come "through / my hand / to / you." Indeed, one strength of the video installation is its power to draw the viewer/reader into its poetics:

exactly

what

i

see

now

i

see

now

This poetic phrase draws the reader into the video not just because of the single-word lines, but also because of its content: like much of *Brush Mind: At Hand*, this is a commentary on time and the body, a kind of speech act. Consider, for example, the significance of these words if they were read aloud. This statement calls attention to the different levels of perception that the "I" is experiencing; this is both a fact and a self-conscious provocation. Drawing attention to the act of seeing in this way is perhaps particularly significant given the medium by which this video is encountered—on a screen, in a world in which screens are understood to distract and splinter consciousness, time, and mental energies rather than focusing them in the way the video does.

The second musical frame of *Brush Mind*, composed and played by Andrew Raffo Dewar, is marked by a mechanical hum of working electronics. This music suspends certainty and is not as mystical as the first musical frame. Some of the notes mimic whale sounds in the way they swing wildly from the top of the musical scale to the bottom. Due to the music alone, this second version is less sure of itself but remains curious, exploring, prodding, poking.

Electronic music which resembles strings and reed instruments
introduces us to the video's third iteration (composed and played by
Holland Hopson) of *Brush Mind: At Hand*. Forest sounds seep in; the
sound of water trickles through a creek, and frogs and insects add a
layer of natural rhythm. A sound like the scraping of a violin adds a
sense of foreboding, resembling an uncannily long human "e" vowel
sound. In each version of the work, musical frames lend variations
in meaning to the words. Thus, when a simple, uncertain chord
frames the fragment "is / this / my / winding / down," the question
becomes sadder than in the first version, in which death is an almost
welcome reality due to the wondrous music framing it. In the third
version, sonar soundings help us navigate "this / moment / is / your
/ life," while the sounds of a creek come back with "the books / the
music / have / a way / of finding me." Running water fades to silence
with the final frame, "pay me / no mind." In the video of *Brush Mind:
At Hand*, the musical frames thus inject different meaning-oriented
intonations into each poetic fragment, making its viewing a complex
emotional, spiritual, and bodily experience. The music in the last
section push us to grapple harder with the writing, whereas the
middle section's ambiguous musical tones cause some productive
discomfort. Meanwhile, the first section is filled with timbres
of wonder. The installation dimensions – of video and musical
compositions – when placed within a quiet gallery or museum
venue (or in a darkened room on a large computer screen) offer an
additional meditative reading opportunity, at once transforming and
re-enforcing the text itself.

    Unlike many texts in the Western Zen tradition, this book
does not require any knowledge of either Judeo-Christian philosophy
nor of Zen—it is welcoming to all readers of English. As the phrase
"through / my hand / to / you" suggests, the handwritten book wants
to engage with the reader, and in turn to ask the reader to engage
with "not these / words exactly / but the / brushing up / against /
something / else." This is a contemplation of language, matter, and
time; mind and body; Western Zen and Judeo-Christian spiritualities;
American colloquialisms and Zen axioms. The poetics of *Brush
Mind: At Hand* allows each of these traditions to breathe in their own
particularities at the same time that the book gathers them together
for a cosmic yet down-to-earth reading experience.

Brush Mind: At Hand, Greencup Books 2016, 64 pages, $9.95, ISBN 978-1-943661-06-0

Video/Installation by Jane Cassidy. Music by Michael Harp/Aaron Dues; Andrew Raffo Dewar; Holland Hopson. (Installation: Sella Granata Art Gallery, Tuscaloosa, AL, October 17-19, 2017.)

Interview with Hank Lazer

Sara Wilson

Brush Mind: at Hand questions asked by Sara Wilson

1. I assume you have worked with Kaz before?

Only in the sense that I have sat *sesshin* with him & heard his dharma talks when I was at the Upaya Zen Center several years ago. I have since studied or learned about Kaz's work via books (one called *Brush Mind*), his superb translations (including the complete *Shobo Genzo* by Dogen – a book that is crucial to my ongoing Notebooks project, beginning with Notebook 31), and a number of video talks and demonstrations. I have not studied calligraphy with Kaz (nor with anyone else). I have had the opportunity to visit his studio in Berkeley.

2. Some of your poetry is delightful in its basic colloquial tone/content. Why the colloquialisms?

As your question implies, I too take delight in the colloquial (though I also take delight in more esoteric or conceptual or philosophical vocabularies too). I admire the fusion of colloquial and philosophical

thinking. I suppose that in some sense, what I'm doing in the Brush
Mind works bears some kinship to the colloquial/philosophical
thinking found in David Antin's talk-poems. (I admired David and
his work a great deal.) I suppose that the colloquial is also a way
to honor my father's thinking. (He was in no way academically or
philosophically inclined, except in a lived and colloquial manner.)
I particularly like it when the colloquial phrase has multiple
resonances, multiple possibilities to it, as in a phrase/page such as
"what's/ it/ to/ you" or "who/ would/ be/ any/ the wiser." I also spend
some part of each week on a farm in a remote part of west central
Alabama, and once again I am in contact with (and admire) a very
down to earth mode of thinking and expression. I like – not only in
Brush Mind, but in my other 25 books of poetry – the collision of the
colloquial with more specialized poetic or philosophical vocabularies.

3. Was this project something you worked into an everyday
schedule; did you treat it like a journal?

Not at all. Gradually, over many months, I began to develop a feel
for the Brush Mind kind of writing as distinct from the shape-writing
of the Notebooks. I would write however many pages/statements
occurred to me certain mornings (that's my usual writing time,
though Brush Mind statements can occur almost anytime of day),
and once I feel like I have enough for a book, I put them in a folder,
and return to them much later. For *Brush Mind: At Hand*, I looked
at many of the initial year's-worth of pages, and I made a selection
of a book-length group of pages. Actually, more than a book-length
selection, and thus the final process involved eliminating pages that
felt less effective or essential or less interesting.

4. I love your writing, and it strikes me as a very idiosyncratic
calligraphic style. What were/are your feelings about your
calligraphy? In the poetry reading at OU, you poked a bit of
fun at it, calling it "childish writing"—but you must be a tad
proud of this as well?

Sure: proud or pleased, yes. While at the same time acknowledging
that there is a roughness to the writing as well. I think of my writing
as calligraphy in the sense that it embraces the moment and

spontaneity. I know that from certain classical perspectives my printing is not "beautiful," and that there is a certain primitive or childish awkwardness to it. But I like those qualities. Not only in my own handwritten work, but especially in Southern folk (or outsider) art, and in plenty of other places where the handwritten pops up (Cy Twombly, for example from the fine art world; JB Murry from the folk-art world).

> 5. *Brush Mind: At Hand* seems to announce itself as a meditative practice, both in its writing and its reading. Is that what it felt like while you were writing?

Yes, though a bit more overtly joyous and amused/amusing...

> 6. You move back and forth between spiritual traditions so easily in *Brush Mind: At Hand*. Was that your experience in writing it—that is, while you were writing, were these spiritual traditions as porous for you as you've made them in the book?

Yes. It's just who I am and where I live... My own spiritual life is based on Jewish and Buddhist and poetic/word practices. And where I live – Alabama – has a rather decidedly Christian emphasis as well, which is something I also find in much of the visionary folk art I admire here too. So, yes, that kind of movement or poly-spirituality comes quite naturally and is not something I have to strive to achieve nor do I work at it as if it were an intention.

> 7. Were you imagining a reader or audience while writing?

No. As usual, I didn't know what I was doing when I began writing the first series for Brush Mind. Norman (Fischer – longtime friend, poet, Zen priest) gave me a soft brush pen and said he'd be curious to see what I did with it. (Norman has written about my shape-writing, and he is very familiar with the Notebooks project.) Brush Mind gradually became my use of this pen. It's only just recently – after 2-3 years of Brush Mind pages of writing – that I begin to understand what sort of form or experience I've come to make in this mode of composing. (More on that in subsequent questions/

answers.)

8. Was there ever a point where as a Westerner, you were intimidated by the long history and tradition of Buddhist practice?

Yes. Always, and never. I know there is so much that I don't know. So, I keep practicing, reading, sitting, learning, listening. I also know that it's fine to proceed as is. So, I do.

9. Collaborating on projects is not new for you, but what does collaboration teach you? Did it teach you anything fresh this time, working with Jane Cassidy, Michael Harp, Aaron Dues, Andrew Raffo Dewar, and Holland Hopson?

Of course. I always learn something new from each collaboration. Sometimes, the learning is rather mundane, as in how long it took to get finished 9:30 compositions/completed tracks from each musician. Or, once we had the music, how quickly we – through Jane Cassidy's video and installation sense – got to have an installation. And how much difference a simple color reversal can make – shifting from the white background and black ink to the video installation version with black background and white writing. With each musician, the work went differently. Michael Harp's piece (which was a collaboration with his friend Aaron Dues, whom I had not met previously) came out of a final project in my undergraduate seminar, Zen Buddhism and Radical Approaches to the Arts. I liked the composition so much that I asked Michael if he could produce a 9:30 version. With Andrew (with whom I have worked before, and have performed jazz-poetry concerts in Athens, Georgia and Havana, Cuba) we met periodically to find an appealing electronic/synthesizer palette of sounds, and Andrew then proceeded with the piece. We would get together every few weeks and go over what music was emerging from our interaction. Holland (with whom I have collaborated previously on a set of multi-voice pieces from my Notebooks - http://www.drunkenboat.com/db22/poetry/hank-lazer) the process was similar – identifying a range of sounds that would become part of the composition. Holland and I also met periodically to listen, react to, and fine tune the emerging composition. These latter two compositions took approximately 6 months to complete. It's also important to know that in no way – with any of the musicians – did we attempt to coordinate the music with each frame of *Brush Mind: At Hand*. The music came out of an overall sense of the book, and once we synchronized the two, there were some pleasant surprises.

> 10. You mentioned you are recently finishing up sequels to *Brush Mind: At Hand*. Can you give us a sense of what these sequels might look like and read like?

As I answer your questions (late January, early February 2018), I was just finishing up *Brush Mind 4: This Moment*. *Brush Mind 2* is subtitled *Second Hand*, and *Brush Mind 3* is called *Hold It*. There is a gentle, peaceful tone – a sense of gratitude – that is essential to *Brush Mind 2*. Many of its pages come out of my recent *sesshin* (7-day meditation retreat) at Mar de Jade, a meditation center in a small fishing village (Chacala, Nayarit) in Mexico, hence the periodic Spanish phrases. (The services at Mar de Jade were conducted mostly in Spanish, with some phonetic reading/chanting in Japanese, with dharma talks being bilingual, English and Spanish). I have only recently begun working with Holland Hopson on the music for *Brush Mind 2*. In keeping with my experience at Mar de Jade, the musical composition will consist (I think) of ocean sounds, of waves breaking. *Brush Mind 3* is a bit darker, more jangly, more a response to these particularly dark and challenging times, and I think that the music for that one will be electric guitar. (I hope to work with guitarist Davey Williams on this one.) And *Brush Mind 4*, which has some of the serenity of *Brush Mind 2*, I hear as having a music consisting of natural sounds – mainly crickets, cicadas, insects, frogs, and similarly textured electronic and percussion sounds, and I plan to work with percussionist Timothy Feeney on that one. I have very recently been in touch the Russell Helms, the publisher of *Brush Mind: At Hand*, and he's eager to embark on the sequels (for which we have some fun design ideas).

> 11. What motivated you to extend the reach of *Brush Mind: At Hand* with a sequel?

I've been gathering and putting in folders many, many Brush Mind pages. Periodically, I gather them together and see what happens. I find the Brush Mind composing to be an interesting complement to my ongoing shape-writing in the Notebooks. And I am very pleased with the production that publisher Russell Helms accomplished with *Brush Mind: At Hand*. The Brush Mind pages that I write at home are on 8 ½ x 11 white (bright thick) paper, and Russell created a perfect match with the book format, with some smart details: writing on only one side of the page; a simple cover, but with a waxy quality so that it isn't easily damaged; and most important of all: CHEAP. (Unit cost under $5.) I am really having great fun now imagining a run of many more Brush Mind compositions, though of course this is being done apart from any demand (for, as best I can tell, the demand for these books is virtually nonexistent).

> 12. What insights have you developed on the nature of these compositions—what has your own work taught you?

It takes (or has taken me) many years to write with (resonant) simplicity. Only recently, after two or three years of writing these pages, I had an intense and fully formed insight into what the Brush Mind composition is. There is the book itself – roughly 64 pages of text. From the installation experience, I now see, hear, and think of each iteration of Brush Mind as being a 10:00 production: 9:30 of music, with 15 seconds of fade at the beginning and ending. Each Brush Mind I now think of as one poem – 64 pages or 10 minutes in duration – and as such as constituting a particular tone (though with counterpoints and interruptions, so as not to be boring or overly didactic). Sort of an extended tone poem, or interval of consciousness. Typically, I begin working initially with more pages – approximately 65-90 pages – than the final composition requires. The pages I use are all from a common time period of writing (sometimes a span of several weeks or months, sometimes as brief as a week or two). I prune the grouping back toward that 64 page goal, and also modify the chronology of the pages. But the resulting form that I'm describing (as the endpoint of the process) begins to be as specific as a sonnet or any other form. There will be one page that has the flash of rays exploding on the page. There will be a page that evokes the Duncan Farm life and language – a 200 acre farm in remote west Alabama, and where we see only a few people, mainly a couple of my wife's cousins, and where the language of the place is wonderfully rich and simple. There will be plenty of colloquial phrases (with multiple resonance). There will be some direct reaching out to the reader/listener, playing with the immediacy of reading and attention. And a few other recurring elements that I am only now beginning to realize.

What has the work taught me? Plenty! A joy in simplicity that I had not expected – a simplicity that I hope still allows for a certain good-humored depth of thinking. An alternate mode of writing while I continue writing the shape-writing Notebooks, and I've learned (slowly) that the mode of writing in Brush Mind also brings with it important continuities with my other writing practices: another (but decidedly different) exploration of the hand-written work; a link to possibilities for collaboration with other media (video, music, installation); and continued investigation of invented (rather than received) forms of composition. At the heart of this writing experience, I've learned, once again, to trust a compelling impulse even though the immediate practice exceeds any kind of conscious intention. To write without knowing what I'm writing, or why.

'In His Rightful Garden':
Anthony Rudolf, the Poet

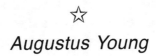

Augustus Young

'The last at last seen by him

himself unseen by him

and of himself'.

Samuel Beckett

All poets are in crisis. The next poem may never come. Rodin calmed Rilke's panic with, 'work, work hard, and exercise patience'. No poet I know is as patient as Anthony Rudolf. Not that he doesn't 'work, work hard', but all too often it is on something else. But the 'patience' has paid off. *European Hours* (Carcanet Press, 2018), his collected poems, is a rounded body of work.

  I first met Anthony Rudolf in the early 1970s at the ICA. He had been convening a symposium on poetics with some well-known critics and poets. Impressed by his assurance and knowingness, I saw him as a wheeler and dealer in Literary London. As we became friend I realized how wrong I was. Rudolf was a mover and shaker of the dream of poetry who, where it was coming true, made his presence felt. He had gained the respect and affection of poets as different as Donald Davie, F.T. Prince, Andre Frenaud and Jon Silkin.

Rudolf opened up the world of books for me, the old and new: Montaigne, Stendhal's non-fiction, Paz, Borges, George Oppen and the Objectivists, Popa and the Eastern Europeans. As a young Irish poet who had only just eradicated the adventitious roots of Yeats, I was overwhelmed. And so was Anthony, I think, to find himself as a translator in collaborating with Yves Bonnefoy, Claude Vigée and Yevgeni Vinokurov. He enthused about their poetry, and never mentioned his own.

'Let me be a garden at whose fountains/ my swarming dreams could pluck new blooms'. Rilke's lines prompted the young poet of the *Letters* to write to him. Hilaire Belloc, a multifaceted author and polemist, regretted that he 'never in my rightful garden lingered'. That is, concentrating on poetry. Anthony Rudolf lies somewhere between Rilke and Belloc (his French side). Rilke who offered himself a life as a pure poet, composing letters and immortal works. Belloc who never stopped writing popular books and unpopular articles for the market, and only moonlighted in poetry.

Apart from his high profile as a translator, Rudolf became internationally recognized as the creative editor of Menard Books, not only publishing poetry and essays, but responding to the nuclear and climate threats with influential pamphlets by renowned experts. At the same time, he was all-purpose literary and political 'boy-scout' organizing reading, meetings and lectures. On top of that, to support a growing family, he had to make a living in the BBC World Service, where his language skills were occasionally put to good use. However, poetry was never far from his sight. While publishing books around and about it, throughout his life he improvised poems and published some of them quietly. Far from being a secondary activity, it was a wholehearted commitment to making poetry out-of-the-ordinary, original and discretely ambitious. Similar in a way to his first-floor garden in his flat at 8 The Oaks, a veranda with flower-pots looking out on neighbors' allotments. It's like being in a Morandi painting.

Collected poems are the graveyard of many a good poet. Deadwood work gets in. Poets I love like Ed Dorn, Edwin Morgan, Christopher Middleton, were diminished by the inclusion of poems that anyone could write. Surplusage is not a problem with Rudolf. There are less than a hundred, averaging two a year, although clearly some years were more productive than others. A wish for more can be countered by a purist case for less. The quality is uneven and some occasional family poems would best be left to the memory book. Less is often more, all the better to appreciate the achieved. Most poets who survive the test of time do so with a handful of poems. True, a study of their less remembered work deepens our understanding of the survivors. They may have a new life with musical settings, or revive interest in a neglected influence, or offer biographical information that throws new light on the well-known poems. Some of Rudolf's poems work like that, and the broader context offered by *European Hours'* supplement of prose excerpts and generous notes is frequently enlightening.

The book begins with the title prose poem. Rudolf has a gift for lists and litotes. It is an understated love poem in which great art is equated with happiness (it's not an either/or as Rilke claimed). The beloved is an artist visiting a litany of European art galleries to look again at paintings that are necessary for her work. Since the book is dedicated to 'Paula Rego at home, in the studio, in Europe', we know the artist is Rudolf's partner. The cover painting (Rego,1997) shows a priestly figure perched on a sofa in a red and black dressing gown looking thoughtful, books strewn around him. Rudolf, as her favorite male sitter of many years, is readily recognizable. The grand tour starts in her studio, and ends in a small chapel in Colmar where in the candle-light the artist's eye catches a fresco of two angels, and takes out her pencil and sketch book, a full circle. It's a love poem like no other unless one matches it with 'Colombine at the Picasso exposition, Paris, November ,1996', which is a more lyrical version of Rego in her element, looking and knowing what she has to see.

Apart from 'European Hours', the poems are presented chronologically. The jacket quotes Ted Hughes, 'Every poem has a new geometry – of surprises. A strange voice of cat's cradles in a Kafkaesque half-light'. The early work from the sixties fits this description best. They are very much of their period (the word 'reify' is a tell-tale) but not period pieces. Two poems stand out. 'Obsession: a structure' and 'Necessary fiction'. A line in 'Obsession' connects them: 'The stone in my head /kicks like an unborn baby'. A sense of the rockface of life that the mind has to climb to reach air pervades these impressively compressed poems.

The hardened heart of rock was still

beating. That I knew, but did not feel.

I had no choice. Stone change is not

on a scale the heart of man

can measure. Reason

is party to this ignorance.

But what if what I know is so much air

when feeling does not lie upon

mind's bedrock? And would what is felt

be necessary fiction

as if it were independent of a thought?

I move the rock. It is not moved.

    European Hours is a book of small crises. Crises of confidences, sometimes in relation to others, sometimes writerly, but always with an existential sting in the tail/tale (puns often are the sub-plot). Anxiety ('Checkpoint Charlie') and memory ('Childhood', 'For all we know') are put to rest, but neither quite opens the door to the life outside, which remains for Rudolf 'a reflection in my words'. The closet feeling of being immured in rock, maybe a metaphor for weighty expectations, is lightened by intellectual limpidity and a mordant wit.

    The poems of his middle period are anticipated with the line 'silence is/ the deepest structure of them all' ('Invisible ink') when stone as the motif is replaced by silence, and the insouciance of his early work becomes more fragmented. A certain *broyer noir* with a dramatized self-pity achieves effective poems ('In his death').

in his death

they let him down

slowly, carefully

into the grave

and shovel earth

over him

to share the blame

as it is said

in his life

they let him down

      Not that the poet has come to a dead-end, but it is close, as a subsequent poem 'The same river twice' implies:

He took my words.

          Without a word

he changed the order of my things.

Still my poems, just about.

Much water has flowed by.

          No word.

But to this day, ten years on

I write the same words.

          The end

of all my words is a beginning.

      There are several false starts ('Word of mouth/ makes nothing happen') until Rudolf on a visit to his Mecca Paris makes a pilgrimage to the garret Rimbaud stayed in, and the door of his mind begins to open:

How shall I know for certain there is no past

to meet with, no future for the dead

poet, save in his writing?

He answers, emboldened by 'The Season in Hell', Rimbaud's last great poem, by inviting himself to dine with his favorite French poet on 'wine, sun, bread, tobacco', and 'there mocked by your silence yes I shall know'.

Having wanted to write 'the history of silence', and faced by
a blank wall, Rudolf finds architecture and more importantly painting,
informed and guided by the love of, and in, his life. The assured step
returns to his poems ('The true inflections', 'Picture at an exhibition').
Not all the poems cohere, until the nineties when the painterly genre
hits its stride. The result is an 'inscape' into an interior world that
has made itself visible, and, as he stands back, his lateral vision
is able to take in the setting that contains it, not least this artist
companion and her professional communion with her colleagues,
past and present. Rudolf is at home here as he was in his literary
youth with eminent poets. He has found the dream of painting come
true, and its embodiment.

Colombine, Picasso Exhibition, Paris November, 1996

She leaves me at the photographs

to reapply

herself to the paintings.

Soon enough, I follow her

to the portrayal

of Salvado dressed as Harlequin.

'See the way Picasso

uses distemper:

I can learn from him'.

I observe

how well she looks

at what

is seen

to be the case in point:

a mirror image.

Rudolf diversified into poems that speak to artists looking at their own paintings: for example, 'The Bread of Faithful Speech' (Pierre Rouve), 'Removal Man', (Natalie Dower), and less successfully with 'Architexture' (Julie Farrer). The last stanza is a heavy statement that spoils the light-tripping that proceeds it. He does not include Rego in this category. Sitters are silent partners.

The final poem is 'Zig-zag', a lesson in autobiography for his students, it's the nearest thing to an extended form in his poetry. A collage of quotations and hard-earned wisdoms, it should be read by anyone who writes. Towards the end, he says, 'nothing will work/ unless you confront/ fear and shame'. And qualifies it with a hesitation. A certain worthiness enters the equation (never write about your children), and the closely argued text loses its grip, reminding me of his lines in 'Removal Man' 'I/ am a fly/ on the wall of your/ mind, set/ against/ disorder…/ I empty my/ head to a vacuum/ that I may leave/ room'. However, it's by no means a Kantian stand-back. He is shrugging off his daemons, and break-dancing out of negative thoughts going nowhere except down. This is a characteristic I've always admired in his temperament. Rudolf knows when to break loose. The poem concludes:

In painting I hear

a harmony, silent
as the great Watteaus
and Poussin's 'A dance
to the Music of Time',

ultrasound seen in
the Wallace Collection.
Then, without speaking,
I walk round the corner

And there in the Wigmore
Hall, I await
(blotting out painting)

whatever music,

for this in which

it tells us is

itself before it

speaks to our condition.

When Anthony Rudolf wrote his own autobiography, *Silent Conversations* (Seagull, 2013), it was as an epic reader. The threads of his life can only be stitched together between the lines of seven hundred pages of deep-felt and delved literary appreciation. His mask is behind a book, and behind the mask there is a smile. Rudolf thinks he's the only one that knows that. He is wrong. In *European Hours* the twinkle can be seen, eye to eye.

Notes on Contributors

Mark Axelrod-Sokolov is a Professor of Comparative Literature in the Department of English at Chapman University, Orange, California, has been Director of the John Fowles Center for Creative Writing and Editor of *Mantissa, the Literary Journal of the John Fowles Center* for 22 years. He has taught screenwriting in numerous countries in the US, UK, Europe and Latin America and has won dozens of fiction and screenwriting awards as well as Fulbright Awards and National Endowment for the Arts grants. He has published extensively in fiction, non-fiction, film and literary criticism. His latest fiction books include *Balzac's Coffee, DaVinci's Ristorante; Dante's Foil & Other Sporting Tales; Café Nietzsche Axel's Charhouse; Bartleby's Books, Gatsby's Café* and the translation of Balzac's play, *Mercadet*, which was retitled, *Waiting for Godeau*. His latest books of literary criticism are *Madness in Fiction: Literary Essays from Poe to Fowles* and his book, *Notions of Otherness: Literary Essays from Cahan to Maraini* were published by Palgrave and Anthem respectively. He adapted his novel, *The Mad Diary of Malcolm Malarkey*, into a screenplay titled, *Malarkey,* starring Malcolm McDowell that is currently with a literary agent in Los Angeles. At last count, he had written over 125 volumes of prose, poetry, drama, film and literary criticism and in 2017 he was inducted into the European Academy of Arts and Sciences, Salzburg.

Ian Brinton's recent publications include a *Selected Poems & Prose of John Riley* and *For the Future,* a festschrift for J.H. Prynne (both from Shearsman Books), a translation of selected poems by Philippe Jaccottet (Oystercatcher Press) and he is working on an autobographical account of teaching English. His translations of Baudelaire and Mallarmé are due to be published later in 2019. He co-edits *Tears in the Fence* and *SNOW* and is involved with the Modern Poetry Archive at the University of Cambridge.

Sarah Hayden: 'S1: Holt' comes from an ongoing series of lecture-poems. This text was first published in Slovak translation by Ivana Hostová in *Vertigo 4* (2018). Readers might want to watch the 1974 video *Boomerang*, which can be viewed at: https://www.youtube.com/watch?v=qc6Meui6GWM

Sarah Hayden's chapbooks are *sitevisit* (Materials, 2018), *Turnpikes* (Sad Press, 2017), *System Without Issue* (Oystercatcher, 2013) and *Exteroceptive* (Wild Honey, 2013). Other poems and lecture-poems have appeared in *para·text, Blackbox Manifold, Golden Handcuffs Review, Tripwire, datableed* and elsewhere. She is the author of *Curious Disciplines: Mina Loy and Avant-Garde Artisthood*, and co-author, with Paul Hegarty, of *Peter Roehr–Field Pulsations.* Her new project is on voiceover in artists' moving image and video art: www.voicesinthegallery.com.

Tania Hershman's third short story collection, **Some Of Us Glow More Than Others**, was published by Unthank Books in May 2017, and her debut poetry collection, *Terms & Conditions*, by Nine Arches Press in July. Tania is also the author of a poetry chapbook, *Nothing Here Is Wild, Everything Is Open*, and two short story collections, *My Mother Was An Upright Piano,* and *The White Road and Other Stories*, and co-author of *Writing Short Stories: A Writers' & Artists' Companion* (Bloomsbury, 2014). Tania is curator of short story hub ShortStops (www.shortstops.info), celebrating short story activity across the UK & Ireland, and has a PhD in creative writing inspired by particle physics. Hear her read her work on https://soundcloud.com/taniahershman and find out more here: www.taniahershman.com

Fanny Howe's most recent books were *The Needle's Eye* and *Second Childhood*, both from Graywolf. In Fall 2019, a collection of her poems called Love and I will be brought out by Graywolf too.

Peter Hughes, currently based in a cabin on the margins of Snowdonia, is a poet, painter and the founding editor of Oystercatcher Press,. He was recently the Judith E. Wilson Visiting Fellow in Poetry at Cambridge University. He lived in Italy for several years and has created innovative versions of classic Italian texts. Publications include a *Selected Poems* (from Shearsman); *Quite Frankly*, versions of Petrarch's sonnets (Reality Street); and *Cavalcanty* (Carcanet). His versions of Leopardi came out from Equipage in 2018 under the title *via Leopardi 21. A Berlin Entrainment*, his most recent book, fruit of time spent in Berlin, is published by Shearsman. The pieces in the current magazine derive from Cant, the Welsh for 100, the English for 'can't', Brexit and the vast blimps of reactionary bullshit that dominate the airwaves and print culture of this small bunch of islands off the west coast of Europe. Each piece consists of 100 words.

Robert C. Jones was born in West Hartford, Connecticut in 1930. Bob died December 23, 2018 in Seattle, Washington. He attended Kenyon College and Rhode Island School of Design, where he studied with John R. Frazier and Robert G. Hamilton, and he worked briefly with Hans Hoffman in Provincetown. He has taught at RISD, the University of Washington, and summers at Sheldon College and the University of British Columbia. Solo exhibitions include the Tacoma Art Museum, Seattle Art Museum's Documents Northwest, Whatcom Museum of History and Art, Museum of Northwest Art, Hallie Ford Museum of Art, and Cornish College of the Arts. In 1990, he was honored with a Western States Arts Federation/National Endowment for the Arts Fellowship, and in 2004 he received a Flintridge Foundation Award for Visual Artists. From 1969 until its closing in 2013, Bob was represented in Seattle by the Francine Seders Gallery. Since 2015, Bob has been represented by G.Gibson Gallery in Seattle.

Longtime UW colleague and painter, Michael Spafford writes: *Robert Cushman Jones was a pure painter and a great inspiration*

for me and many others. When I look at his work, I see symphonies.
He composed visual music with shifting tonalities, shapes and colors.
I can almost hear what I see. When artists of his brilliance die, the
whole world suffers. My eyes are full of tears.

Daphne Marlatt immigrated to Vancouver, Canada from Penang, Malaysia with her family in 1951. She is a critically acclaimed poet and novelist whose cross-genre work has been translated into French and Dutch. The bicultural production of her Canadian Noh play, *The Gull*, received the 2008 international Uchimura Naoya Prize. Recent poetry titles include **Liquidities: Vancouver Poems Then and Now** (2013) and Intertidal: Collected Earlier Poems 1968-2008, edited by Susan Holbrook. The poems in this issue respond to excerpts from letters her father wrote in the 1930s from Penang where he went to work as a chartered accountant.

Jake Marmer is a poet, performer, and educator. He is the author of *The Neighbor Out of Sound* (2018) and *Jazz Talmud* (2012), both published by the Sheep Meadow Press. Jake writes about poetry for *Tablet Magazine* and teaches high school. Born in the provincial steppes of Ukraine, in a city which was renamed four times in the past 100 years, he considers himself a New Yorker, even though he lives in the Bay Area.

Toby Olson's new book of poems, *Death Sentences*, will appear in the coming months from Shearsman Press

Kat Peddie is a lecturer in Creative Writing at the University of Kent. Her pamphlet of Sappho translations and variations, *Spaces for Sappho*, came out with Oystercatcher in 2016, and is part of a larger and ongoing project of 'translating' Sappho. She has published translations, poetry, photography and criticism in various publications, including Shearsman, Tears in the Fence, Litmus, Snow, Molly Bloom, Litter, Junction Box, Tentacular and Datableed magazines. She also helps to run the art, activism and community space the Temporary Centre for Resistance at the University of Kent as part of the Kent Precariat, and gigs regularly with Free Range Orchestra, an improvisatory music and movement ensemble. She mainly writes, and writes on, love poems, translation, collage, gender and sexuality.

Meredith Quartermain's work can be found in Best Canadian Poetry 2018 and 2009. Her first book, *Vancouver Walking*, won a BC Book Award for Poetry, and her second book, *Nightmarker* was a finalist for a Vancouver Book Award. Other books include *Recipes from the Red Planet* (finalist for a BC Book Award in fiction); *I, Bartleby: short stories*; and *U Girl: a novel*. From 2014 to 2016, she was Poetry Mentor in the SFU Writer's Studio Program, and in 2012 she was Vancouver Public Library Writer in Residence.

British poet **Aidan Semmens's** fourth collection, *Life Has Become More Cheerful*, was published by Shearsman Books in 2017 on the centenary of the Russian Revolution. Previous titles include *The Book of Isaac* (Parlor Press 2013) and *Uncertain Measures* (Shearsman 2014). He also edits the online magazine *Molly Bloom*. www.aidansemmens.co.uk

Alan Singer is the author of five novels, most recently *The Inquisitor's Tongue* (FC2, 2013). "Audience" is excerpted from his recently completed novel *Play, A Novel*. Alan Singer is also the author of five scholarly books, most recently *Posing Sex: Toward a Perceptual Ethics for Literary and Visual Art* (Bloomsbury, 2018). He is on the faculty of English and Creative Writing at Temple University.

Marilyn Stablein, poet, essayist, fiction writer and mixed media artist whose collage, assemblages, sculptural artist's books, and performance art explore and document visual narrative, travelog and memoir. Her last book was *Vermin: A Traveler's Bestiary* (Spuyten Duyvil). Two books published in 2019: *Houseboat on the Ganges & A Room in Kathmandu: Letters from India & Nepal 1966-1972* (Chin Music Press); *Milepost 27: Poems* (Black Heron Press). Visit: marilynstablein.com

Philip Terry is a translator, and a writer of fiction and poetry. He has translated the work of Georges Perec, Stéphane Mallarmé and Raymond Queneau, and is the author of the novel *tapestry*, shortlisted for the Goldsmiths Prize. His poetry volumes include *Oulipoems, Shakespeare's Sonnets, Dante's Inferno, Quennets, Bad Times* and *Dictator*, a version of the *Epic of Gilgamesh*. He is currently translating Ice Age signs.

Sara Wilson is a PhD candidate in literary and cultural studies at the University of Oklahoma with interests in twentieth-century American and transpacific poetry and poetics. She has taught at Beijing Normal University, the University of Oklahoma, Northern Virginia Community College, and American University.

Lissa Wolsak is a poet, goldsmith and Master of Energy Psychology presently living in Langley, B.C. She is the author of *The Garcia Family Co-Mercy; Pen Chants, or nth or 12 Spirit-like Impermanences; A Defence of Being; An Heuristic Prolusion; Squeezed Light: Collected Works 1995 – 2004* and *Of Beings Alone* which won the bpNichol Award in 2015. The complete long-poem *Of Beings Alone: The Eigenface* was recently published by TinFish Press, and *LIGHTSAIL* from Xexoxial Editions. In the works for late 2019/2020 is the likelihood of an extended collaboration and two-way interview with the visual artist, philosopher and psychoanalyst Bracha Lichtenberg Ettinger.

Augustus Young was born in Cork, Ireland, in 1943, and now lives in a port town on the border between France and Spain. His most recent publications are *The Credit*, reissued as an opera in search of its music, *Duras/Menard, 2018: Heavy Years inside the head of a health worker, Quartet Books, 2018: The Invalidity of all Guarantees: a duologue between Walter Benjamin and Bertolt Brecht* (Labyrinth Books, December 2016): *M.emoire* (Duras/ Menard, 2014), *Diversifications: Poems and Translations* (Shearsman, 2009), and *The Nicotine Cat and Other People: Chronicles of the Self* (New Island/ Duras, 2009). Webzine is www.augustusyoung.com.

Introducing ... grand**IOTA**

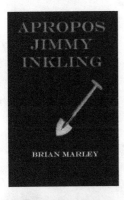

Brian Marley
APROPOS JIMMY INKLING

In a Westminster café-cum-courtroom, Jimmy Inkling is on trial, perhaps for his life. Unless, of course, he's dead already. But will that be enough to prevent him from eliminating those who give evidence against him? "This is a wild, lysergic riff on that hoary staple, the courtroom drama, which, for better or worse, Marley makes his own."
– JG Ballard [attrib.]

978-1-874400-73-8 318pp $13.50 (US) £10 (UK)

Ken Edwards
WILD METRICS

1970s London: short-life communal living, the beginnings of the alt-poetry scene, not forgetting sex, drugs and rock'n'roll. Forty years on: where have the wild metrics of those days taken us? This prose extravaganza dives into the inscrutable forking paths of memory, questions what poetry is, and concludes that the author cannot know what he is doing. Some names have been changed.

978-1-874400-74-5 244pp $13.50 (US) £10 (UK)

grand**IOTA** *is a new initiative of Brian Marley and Ken Edwards, dedicated to imaginative prose writing. We aim to publish books that are out of the ordinary, hard to categorise but good to read.*

You can order books from our website or from your favourite online or offline retailer. Please visit for up to date news and to go on the mailing list.

www.grandiota.co.uk

Meridian
Nancy Gaffield

Between 2015 and 2017, Nancy Gaffield walked the UK's 270-mile Greenwich Meridian Trail from Peacehaven to Sand le Mere, in order to investigate the way that landscapes are disturbed and reordered by history and memory. In *Meridian,* the line of longitude is the 'zero point' through which these forces speak: the intersecting planes of poetry and song, politics and the *polis,* land and sea, presence and absence, shadow and light.

'Nancy Gaffield's bravely resourceful long poem takes us 'true North' with her along the variegated trails marking England's portion of the Meridian. Her lithe, varied poetic lines embody the present and the historic, the minute and the gargantuan, the simple and the complex, the everyday and the artistic, the expected and the surprising – the physical, mental, and emotional experience of her explorations. Combining meditations, reactions, observations, memories with striking ideas, inspired descriptions, literary recalls, the poem captures everything from dirt to ecology to philosophy. Readers will prize this important, inspiring book: the Line, lines, a life brilliantly fused.'
—*Lou Rowan*

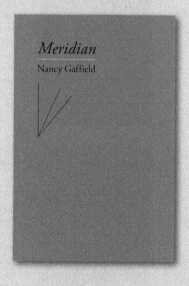

Available now in hardback from Longbarrow Press

Meridian website:
www.ngmeridian.wordpress.com

www.longbarrowpress.com

Longbarrow Press

CPSIA information can be obtained
at www.ICGtesting.com
Printed in the USA
FSHW011158260519
58463FS

9 780990 950684